Isabel's Starry Night

The Magical Quest for Alchemy

Written by

Wanda Webster & Richard M.

Isabel's Starry Night The Magical Quest for Alchemy

Second Edition 2023

www.dynamicsofrecovery.com

info@dynamicsofrecovery.com

YouTube: The Journey Within With Christopher Mack

Podcast: Dynamics of Recovery: From Trauma to Transformation

Companion Book:
The Journey Within, How to create the dynamic of recovery to transform your habits and become your authentic self
Written by Wanda Webster & Christopher Mack

Available on Amazon and Barnes & Noble

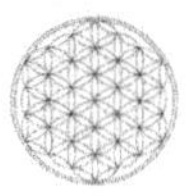

Editorial Praise

The authors did a fantastic job of bringing each character to life, making them feel real and relatable. From the quirky individuals Isabel meets on her journey to the important relationships with her family, I was fully invested in each character's story. – OnlineBookClub

What I loved most about Isabel's Starry Night is the message it conveys. It's a reminder that even when life seems uncertain, we all have the power to transform our lives and find our inner peace. The journey Isabel takes is a reminder to never give up and always keep searching for the light in the darkest places. - OnlineBookClub

Overall, Isabel's Starry Night is a beautiful and magical book that I would highly recommend to anyone searching for answers and meaning in life. The author's storytelling is captivating, and the lessons learned along the way are truly inspiring. It's a must-read for anyone on a journey of self-discovery. - OnlineBookClub

I rate this book **5 out of 5 stars**. It contained a lot of great lessons, and there was nothing to dislike about it. It was professionally edited, as I found one error. I recommend this book to people who enjoy books about self-discovery.

5.0 out of 5 stars A Captivating Journey of Self-Discovery and Transformation. Reviewed in the United States on March 2, 2023 Isabel's Starry Night took me on an incredible journey of self-discovery and transformation. As someone who has struggled to find my place in the world, I immediately connected with Isabel's character. Her journey to find answers and meaning in life was relatable, and the obstacles she faced along the way were both unique and unforgettable.

This book talked about different things pertinent to humans in ways that can be easily understood. Wonderful!

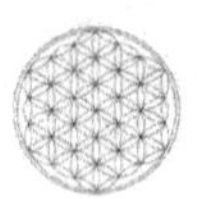

Isabel's journey of self-discovery is eye-opening. Readers would learn from the ways Isabel adapted in order to find her purpose and to rise above her limitations. Totally worth it! Flawless work!!

As an art fan, I liked that this book concentrated on art, particularly Vincent Van Gogh. He was a gifted artist who suffered from a mental disease that most people assumed was bi-polar disorder. In an asylum, he created some of his most famous works. I had never heard of him before reading this book, but I found it fascinating.

I loved reading about Johnny Appleseed, a legendary pioneer who traveled around America sowing apple seeds. Although I had seen the Disney animation centered around him, learning more about this amazing man who had significant influence on America's history was intriguing.

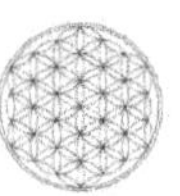

Dedications

This book is dedicated to all the courageous people who constantly strive to improve conditions for themselves and others and who try their best to ease another's pain. To the Change Makers of the world, those who see a better vision for our future, and to all those who wish to learn how.

And thank you, Christopher Mack. You embody all that is kind, right, and noble in this world. I could not have a better partner in life.

~ Wanda Webster

Thank you, Jennifer. You are my grace and my blessing. My loving, patient (oh so patient) wife, sounding board, parachute, early warning system, safety net, best friend, lovely girlfriend, brilliant artist, great human being, modest to a fault, honest, mother to our clan and really, really pretty. Never was there a luckier ER patient.

Dr. Susannah Castle: you have been my caring, brilliant, "cornerman." Whether I am being throttled by a brutish opponent, by reality, or by myself, you have always been in my corner; to steady me, close my wounds, help me catch my breath, focus me and above all give me the strength to go on in my constant fight against the world. ~ Richard M.

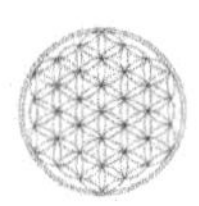

Nirmāna

by Alixen Pham © August 2022

We enter this world through earthlight, strange hands catching
us as we fall from warm darkness into the cold belly of life.
Our mother's voice foretells our destiny: *Babe, Sweetling,*

*Child of pain and desire. All my hopes, all my longings
I bequeath to you.* This shapes the map of our feet, the needs
of our grasp, heart a fretful creature hungry for morsels

of identity, of purpose, of belonging. We exhaust our lives
searching the great expanse, listen to every mouth, sacrifice
to Ra and Yahweh, Shiva to Allah, Jesus and the digital

god's merciless eyes. Anything to not be alone in the chasm
of our deficiencies. Endless voices gnaw at our mind, goading
us to stumble through relationships and addresses like drunkards

gorged on fear and frustrations. Our prayers return to us, stamped:
Undeliverable. Address unknown. After unnumbered starless
seasons, the agony of our longing scours us like wind and water,

polishing layers of dead flesh, distorted beliefs, embers of the past
that crooked our back and blighted our sight, until finally—
call it exhaustion, call it surrender, call it wisdom—Something©

within sirens us. Recalls us to our origins, when each cell of our
being knew itself, its purpose, its source of light in the gradient
womb of blackness. It lulls us back to the sweet shell of our self,

feel the wings of our clavicles, how the universe sings our name
as blessing, the beautiful and fiery breath of Om, a being wrought
with flaring eyes. The tiny smile of awakening dances on our lips.

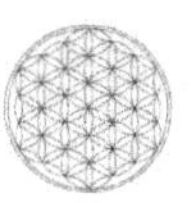

Table of Contents

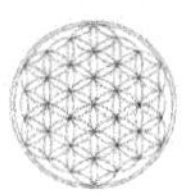

Preface

This story is a work of fiction. The names, characters, places, and incidents either are a product of the authors' imagination or are used fictitiously, and any resemblance to actual persons, living or dead, businesses, companies, events, or locales is entirely coincidental, with the exception of the following:

The various food festivals and Lummi Tribe exist; however, the storyline and characters are fictional. We attempted to depict the tribe's culture and traditions with respect, truth, and dignity to the best of our ability.

The Urban Voices Project is an actual non-profit organization; the characters are depicted with their permission. The storyline of Isabel, however, is fictional as she interacts with these characters.

Although Jim Peters is the mayor of the lovely town of Adel, Iowa, the story is fictional, revolving around our character, Isabel. As well, Dan and Uta Norenberg have given their permission to use their likeness in our fictional story.

Make sure to visit Big Al's BBQ if you travel through Adel, Iowa. It's real and the BBQ is great.

CHAPTER ONE

Do You Believe in Magic?

Isabel Hotchkiss woke up at 10 A.M. She lay there quietly, not moving. She planned to roll out of bed, get dressed, go downstairs, have as much coffee, and as little contact with her family as possible. She needed to tie up any loose ends for her trip and work on "Van Go," her 1955 Harvester International Metro van. Her thought immediately went to, '*What could possibly go wrong?*'

In a much, much former life, her Metro van had been an Alpenrose Dairy milk truck that used to rumble and clatter down suburban Portland streets, leaving a milky, watery trail that the neighborhood cats appreciated. The original looked like a white bulbous Volkswagen van puffed up like a balloon, twice as big as the original VW, with none of those nifty little clerestory-type windows near the roof line. When most people under fifty saw it, their first thought was that it might be a super-sized Volkswagen van. Isabel loved correcting the assumptions and sharing the Metro van's backstory.

It still looked like a milk delivery truck, but under the hood. Ah! Under the hood! Thanks to her mother and father's time, money, and skills, it was a hybrid gas/electric, mostly battery-powered, state-of-the-art vehicle. The van would draw a lot of attention because Isabel painted the outside of it with her favorite painting of all time, her rather impressive version of *Starry Night* by Vincent Van Gogh. Hence the admittedly corny/ almost daddy joke name, "Van Go."

She was pulling on her overalls when she remembered something else. It was her birthday. "Dang!" she quietly growled. "Drat, Gosh Darn!" She stopped and was annoyed that she was already annoyed this early in the morning. She sat on her bed, listening for any movement or shuffling downstairs that would indicate her mother was doing something to prepare for exactly what she *didn't* want.

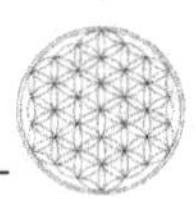

It should be noted that celebrations, especially birthdays, were a tradition in the Hotchkiss family. As far as Philip, her father and master chef, was concerned, any notable event was worthy of a culinary celebration. For Philip, love was any celebration shared; the best thing to share was food, great food, glorious food! Lovingly prepared meals created and given from the heart were what Philip called "kitchen alchemy" because of how they transformed the energy of any celebration.

The food of the holidays (any holiday) was the primary focus of Philip's culinary visions and challenges. Preparing and creating feasts for Christmas, Thanksgiving, the 4th of July, and Easter was a given. But it did not end there. Nope. Not by a long shot. Philip found inspiration in a cornucopia of religious celebrations involving food, some religious, some national, some International, and some historic. His favorite motto about Jewish holidays was made by the character played by Laura San Giacomo (Flo Applebaum) in the essentially obscure and unknown comedy film, *Checking Out*, starring Peter Falk. "All Jewish holidays could be summed up in nine words. They tried to kill us. We won. Let's eat!"

He was about to launch into creating an ultimate gourmet waffle latke with smoked salmon and creme fraiche when "Zitui buns", the focal point and symbol of the Chinese celebration of "Tomb Sweeping Day," grabbed his ADHD/OCD curiosity. He was a master pastry chef, having won the prestigious James Beard Pastry Award and a silver medal in the Asian Pastry Cup awards for superior pastry design in Asia, so there were few things that intimidated Philip. The reporter from Cake magazine said that his Zitui buns "looked like Easter eggs on acid!" It was closer to the truth than they knew.

Despite her father's joyous food-related festivals, Isabel's 21st birthday was a celebration she strongly requested her parents not carry out. No cake. No gifts, no cards, a non-event. When she demanded the non-birthday, she had been quite adamant about it, giving them many reasons, such as the state of the world and the state

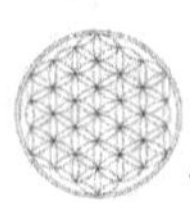

of her hometown of Portland, Oregon, after the multiple pandemic restrictions. There was also the escalating homelessness, graduating college with honors, as she called it, "Summa cum Nada" and "student debt which will keep me financially enslaved for about 130 years."

Benjamin, her younger brother, and a Gen Z Zoomer, called Isabel a "Doomer."

Two months ago, he rolled the "Doomer" stink bomb into her foxhole in front of their mom and dad. Isabel told him to go to hell, but a shrapnel of truth drew blood. It's the label given to people worried about a random list of global crises like overpopulation, worsening climate change, dying oceans, dying coral reefs, dying, generally anything and everything.

She prepared a clever workaround, anticipating this same attack from Benjamin regarding her request for a non-birthday two weeks ago.

"Mom, Dad, I'll admit I'm worried about so many things going on in the world. But there's one thing I'm mostly concerned about: the present and future life of one Isabel Maria Hotchkiss! You are also right, Mom and Dad, I don't know what I want, and I truly need this time to figure it out. I love you, and I know you love me. Perhaps some small birthday celebration when I get back would make more sense. I will have a clear mind, well at least clearer, and be able to appreciate a celebration."

Isabel turned away from them and made sure Benjamin saw her middle finger. As she made her dramatic exit, she saw her parents cock their heads in puzzled bewilderment. The expressions on their faces reminded her of what it would look like trying to explain String Theory to two otherwise intelligent German Shepherds. Isabel knew her parents were more intelligent than German Shepherds, especially her mother (Elizabeth), was brilliant; she had not one, but two PhDs?! Talk about an overachiever. She believed her mom understood string theory considering she taught it at MIT. But her birthday request? *'Nope,'* Isabel thought, *'She definitely has a mom brain that is*

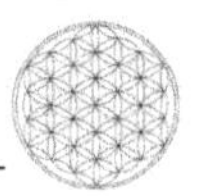

separate from her Ph.D. brain, and that mom brain has love and Mama Bear entanglements in it.'

After Isabel insisted, "No celebration, no presents, nothing!", her parents' reaction gave her a weird power and control to see how unhappy it made them. It dawned on her that she was developing that annoying insight that budding maturity drops on your doorstep as silently as an Amazon package and makes itself known at about 21 years of age, replacing the scorched-earth self-righteousness of a 16-year-old. Isabel noted with irony that the annoying insights into one's maturity are equally as annoying and quite unsettling because she had the tiniest inkling that perhaps her parents were not the cause of all her problems.

Isabel also realized that as a recently hatched quasi-adult, she was on a collision course with her family as she felt the pressures of life and her forthcoming road trip with her beloved van, which needed new tires. She had just graduated and was permitted to explore a few different states throughout the country. *'Maybe I should have asked for those new tires,'* she thought. A wistful voice inside her remembered how they used to be so good at knowing how she felt. Now, they didn't seem to get it, to 'get' her in any way, shape, or form. To be honest, she didn't 'get' herself anymore, either.

'So today, I hit the big milestone, 21.' Isabel thought, *'I can now legally drink, so, therefore I'm an official adult. They will deny it, but I know that in my parent's hearts (and not even that deep in their hearts or minds), they consider me, at best, still a college student, at worst, a teenager. The fact that part of my brain still feels like a college student doesn't help. And I admit that there's a possibility that they don't recognize or respect my adulthood because, even though it was mature and practical to save money by living with them this summer, I'm still in the very same room I've lived in for 21 years.'*

It was true. Other than college, Isabel has existed in the same room almost her entire childhood and has slept in the same bed she's had since she was twelve when she had a pathetic growth spurt of 4 inches up to a towering 5'4". Granted, it's a fantastic bed. (She actually took the mattress to college with her). Seriously, it's a great bed.

It was the same bed where she had done her homework and school projects, talked, texted (incessantly), watched and posted on TikTok and Instagram, and shopped (chiefly for books and overalls, Duluth or Carhartt). Those were the extent of her fashion statement, including her Carhartt knitted Watch Hat.

It was where she wrote her stories, poems, and her honest, sometimes funny, sometimes furious opinion column for her high school paper, "YGTBKM!", (which she carried over to her college blog-YGTBFKM!) Her mother once joked that Isabel's first words were, "You've got to be kidding me?!"

It was the same bed in which she had wept over a boy named Cody, and, later, a girl named Lauren, and then a boy named Austin and one named Grady (who broke up with her because then, requesting 'they' as a pronoun was still, 'working things out.'

The bed was her private island where she first devoured Spotify, YouTube, TikTok, Instagram, and WeChat. And when she was much younger, all Harry Potter books, blogs, newsletters, etc. That all ended abruptly with J.K. Rowling's shocking, heartbreaking, and wrong-minded betrayal of the LGBTQ community. Isabel did not like to 'cancel' anyone, but she did not know what else to do. J.K was canceled in Isabel's mind and her world for now. As it did with so many people who loved Harry Potter, J.K. Rowling broke her heart. She had always wondered why it was so difficult for people to celebrate the uniqueness of each individual. The world could be strangely cruel.

And now, here she was, on her birthday, in bed where she was listening intently for any movement, quick shuffling, or lowered voices from downstairs—listening for anything that would indicate her mother and father were plotting something. After all, they had a history of making glorious cakes for birthdays and celebrations. But she only heard a knock on her door and footsteps quickly receding.

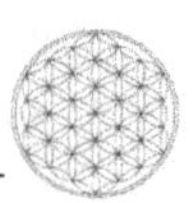

She crossed the room and saw the note someone had slipped under the door.

Isabel opened it and recognized the font from her father's Smith Corona typewriter.

Dear Izzy! We have a problem. As you know, if it is your b***** and if the appropriate b******* celebrant does not choose where to go for a b******* dinner, the next youngest person chooses.**

I hope you would find it in yourself to save me from eating at Benjamin's ridiculous choice: Clowney's Pizza.

GACK!

Your beloved Papa

Isabel was both irritated and amused by the 'trap.' Getting her to celebrate her birthday with a 'casually, going-out-to-dinner-at-a-restaurant' gambit. She felt like she was in an emotional chess game, trying to figure out her parents' next move.

She texted her father:

Thank you for being so considerate (smiley face)

As far as Clowney's Pizza- It's a hard PASS

IMO You should reject his choice based on health reasons alone, both sanitary and quality.

If you do go, I recommend you stick with a salad and garlic knots, and you'll survive (please check on your most recent tetanus shot)

I'll stay here. Thanks, your now 21-year-old daughter

Isabel knew that her rejection of a birthday celebration of any sort, especially this milestone birthday of a Hotchkiss-McMillan firstborn, put a thick wet blanket of gloom over the entire family. But to be fair, Isabel had felt this blanket of gloom for years, and it was only getting worse. She wondered why more people did not feel the dread, despair, and helplessness she felt every time she listened to the news or watched so many injustices played out in the world. She was smart enough to know that everyone faced challenges and that life was not fair, but in this day and age, it felt different. The whole world felt chaotic. How could she possibly celebrate anything and feel good about it?

Isabel took a deep breath and decided to go downstairs to confront the discord she knew she had caused. On the way downstairs, she ran over possible scenarios and types of apologies she might use and still maintain her steadfast desire not to celebrate anything. She startled her parents as she walked through the living room into the dining room. They wheeled around and looked at her with quite guilty looks plastered on their faces. They were also obviously trying to hide something on the dining room table.

"What's wrong?" Isabel asked.

She moved in to get a look at what they blocked from view.

"It is not that serious, honey...." her dad said.

The worry in his voice told her two things; something got screwed up, or they were afraid she'd fly off the handle as she used to when she was a kid. They immediately deflated and stepped aside.

Isabel looked at the table and saw what appeared to be a small green suitcase (made of cake and frosting) with the number 21 meticulously painted on it. The cake was resting on a large round platter with a map of the United States pasted on it and a card that said *Safe Travels*. Isabel didn't know whether she was heartbroken, angry, sad, or frustrated.

She decided she was all those things. (Although she also thought that her dad had designed a magnificent 'safe travels/birthday' cake.) She decided she needed to immediately get out of the house to show that the now mature Isabel did not get as childishly pissed off as she used to. She knew this was also childish but not as immature as screaming about the pseudo-birthday cake.

The Van Go escape was blocked and caused her even more annoyance, anger, and frustration, and besides, she was not sure if she had fully charged the batteries. If only she could calm down. Asking to take one of her parent's cars would not only be uncool, but

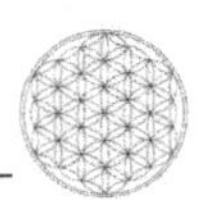

they would probably tell her no because she was upset and shouldn't drive. And, of course, that would get her even angrier, which would prove their point and get her even more frustrated.

That meant taking the 51 bus, which stopped at her corner and went to downtown Portland. Isabel was the type of person who needed a destination, especially when she didn't want to think about something. She had not been downtown in a few years for several reasons: COVID, the never-ending riots, working overtime, fixing up Van Go, and taking a firm hermit-like stance on most social activities.

Isabel took a deep breath and muttered, "I just need some time to myself." As she was walking out the door, Benjamin yelled, "Don't forget your gas mask! You never know when you might need it!"

Upon boarding the bus, she was immediately annoyed because she forgot her pass and had to pay cash. She took another deep breath and tried to gain some inner peace. She settled in her seat and relaxed. The bus passed many familiar houses, but she realized that half the families she knew once lived there were no longer there. She saw very young mothers walking with children on the sidewalks. Some looked like they were only a little older than she was. One of them just might have been Lena Simmons, who was only two grades ahead of her at Lincoln High School. But the woman wore shades and some very Lululemon-ish Yoga clothing while pushing a baby carriage and chatting with two other young mothers pushing expensive-looking carriages. So, Isabel couldn't get her mind around whether it was Lena Simmons or not by the time they had passed by. "Yikes," Isabel said under her breath. The whole thing shook her, and she didn't know why. "But that's the problem; it's everything, isn't it?"

Her thoughts went to her upcoming trip and her last-minute preparations. She would wait till she got out of town to fill the propane tanks. It would be cheaper that way. She also debated whether Van Go's exterior mural needed another clear paint coat. She decided against it. Once again, she checked her itinerary on her phone with all the food festivals along the chosen route, even though she pretty much knew them by heart. She imagined Van Go on the road and how she would be able to show off the interior and the prototype engine developed by her mother, Dr. Elizabeth McMillan.

Mom kept her maiden name, deciding that McMillan-Hotchkiss had far too many consonants. She was a professor of electrical engineering at Oregon State University and an inventor. Dr. McMillan could build just about anything. Like swapping Van Go's underpowered, flathead six-cylinder gas engine with a state-of-the-art electric power plant (which could reach 95 mph). Her mom made her swear never to go over the speed limit, but after Isabel's first speeding ticket, she put a governor on the engine!

There were lots of other electronic goodies in Van Go that her mom installed. A small retractable cell phone tower improved Van Go's Wi-Fi. Solar panels on the roof and friction transfer brakes turned the heat from its brake rotors into usable electric energy. Elizabeth had insisted that Isabel help her build the engine, the transfers, and the solar panels on the roof so she could fix and maintain all of it.

A very cool feature that Isabel installed on the roof was the ear-splitting chrome air horns which she had also promised her mom and dad not to use in the neighborhood or any place else except on the freeway. "Unless you are about to be run over by a log truck," her dad clarified.

Someone once said, "A successful marriage consists of a 'hippie' and a 'cop.' Dr. McMillian was the organized and practical one, the 'cop.' Isabel's dad, the 'hippie,' was exactly the opposite, an inventive risk-taking culinary artist. He could cook just about anything with finesse, perfection, and joy. He was famous for delivering edible delights in a multitude of cuisines from the window of his food truck. His small four-wheeled vehicle, "Starry, Starry Bites," ultimately became Isabel's beloved Van Go.

As the bus arrived in downtown Portland, Isabel was shocked and confused at what she saw. She had been taking the 51 bus along this exact route for 21 years, yet she wasn't exactly sure where she was

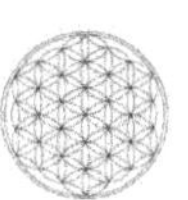

now. It certainly wasn't the same Portland you used to see from the Vista Bridge.

The small, orderly downtown that Portland was so famous for, an urban study on how to plan a city that prided itself on its walkability, was a disaster. The city planners and officials must have looked the other way at how much had been demolished and built in such a short time. Isabel saw mostly high-rise apartments and dozens of even higher-rising, anonymous office buildings, many still under construction.

It reminded Isabel of when she visited San Francisco as a freshman in high school, before the billion-dollar computer tech tsunami hit, and then as a college senior after greed had struck the city by the Bay. The greed swept out any warmth and grace and replaced it with a blade-like skyline, a contemptuous obliteration of scale with bleak, harsh chrome, and glass.

She was starting to regret the decision to come downtown. The bus passed Pioneer Square, once called 'The Living Room' of Portland. Now, homeless people filled the living room. It seemed that ragged transients were everywhere, in the doorways of exclusive department stores and restaurants, milling around the open brick square, setting up tents in every park, grassy exit, and entrance ramp. Every underpass and greenway was staked out in tents and those ubiquitous dark blue tarps, some begging what few tourists remained for a bum cigarette or any spare change.

The bus was finally about to pass the ultimate "bougie," luxury Ritz-Carlton Hotel. Isabel gasped. What had been there before, what had been a considerable part of her life and that of every citizen in Portland, especially the students, was gone! It was all gone. Isabel's excuse for her ignorance was that she was away at college. Her denial machine worked very well, too; she did not want to know. At times, she even fooled herself into ignorance. She secretly wondered if that modus-operandi would continue working now that she was 21.

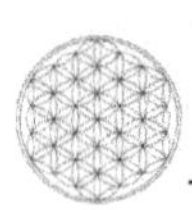

To be built, the owners of the Ritz-Carlton had ejected over 200 food carts from the 3 square blocks that made food carts famous and a vital part of the economy in Portland. It's even in the history books about Portland. Wikipedia will tell you that in the early 1990s, between 9th, 10th, and 11th avenues and Alder and Washington Streets, a few food cart/truck pioneers (including Isabel's dad) built what became Portland's most extensive and longest-running Food Cart Pods. The pioneering Food Pod was known all over the country. Many believe that the Pod finally made Portland a destination city. The Rose Garden did not cut it. Neither did the dragon races or the naked midnight bicycle ride through downtown Portland.

For almost 20 years, a hungry person had the choice of everything from burritos to burgers, Szechuan fried rice to red beans and rice, vegetarian, vegan, Paleolithic, Israeli, Italian, Islamic, Iranian, Chinese, Korean, and Japanese. It was the United Nations of food. The colorful carts, signs, and loud bustle of the crowds made it feel like the circus had come to town. Isabel felt and saw first-hand how the energy transformed the place into something magical called Portlandia.

Starry Starry Bites, with dad at the stove, was voted five years running the best food cart/truck in Portland, and that was saying a lot. Dad's gregarious personality had a lot to do with it. Although even if he had been one of those grumpy, impatient, "I'm bitter and trapped in a food truck" dudes, there would still have been a line down the street because of his magnificent fusions: Asian/Jewish deli food, like Pho beef grinders, ramen carbonara, and Philip's homemade cured pastrami and kimchi. This combo became the Kim-strami fried rice dish. This combo was slightly less popular than his fried turkey wings with 'General Tso What?', a unique sweet and sour orange/cranberry glaze.

General Tso What? Turkey Wings won first prize at the Foster Farms, Turlock, California Turkey Trot Festival. That was the first

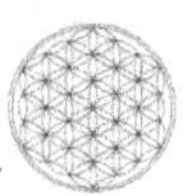

food festival her dad ever took Isabel to, and she became hooked ever since. It was also why she planned her trip to food festivals in various parts of America she hadn't yet seen.

Sitting on the bus watching a disjointed, harsh, new Portland go by, witnessing the changes to the gentle, humanly scaled city Isabel once knew, began to feel suffocating. Isabel had seen enough and remembered enough.

Then she saw another fatality across the street from where the Ritz-Carlton once stood. Alder Gallery, the art gallery where she and her father had met the extraordinary, talented artist Julie Green, was boarded up.

Julie Green had become internationally known for her heart-wrenching, deeply felt "Last Supper" plates which were paintings made on simple white ceramic plates depicting the last meal of almost 1,000 condemned men. Julie created them to protest the United States allowing executions of the convicted (sometimes wrongly) to continue. Green said that through the simple yet powerful energy of the plates, she hoped to use art to convey the fact that these condemned individuals were human beings who, at the end of their life, were making a last, very human choice.

Isabel remembered how her dad excitedly described meeting Ms. Green through her visits to his food truck. Julie struck up a conversation with him and asked if he would design a couple of last meals that condemned inmates requested. Dad had eagerly prepared two or three of the meals. After he mentioned that he used to be a pastry chef, she asked him to bake a birthday cake for someone on death row who had never had one. Dad agreed and said afterward that it simply broke his heart. Then he realized that Julie was sending out a powerful message even though it ended tragically. Dad said he must have cried for half the day for that man who had never seen the joy of people celebrating his birth.

Julie said that she understood and part of it hurt her heart as well to paint the last meals of these human beings. "But we must do it.

We have to break open people's hearts to find enough compassion in them to end these horrible, senseless killings that solve nothing and never have." Julie explained that she hoped her art could facilitate a heart-opening in people, allowing for more empathy, love, and compassion for the human spirit and all sentient beings. Julie quoted the man known only as Dodinsky, "To strengthen the muscles of your heart, the best exercise is lifting someone else's spirit whenever you can."

It seemed logical, bitterly logical, to Isabel that the gallery was obliterated by the same values that destroyed sections of her hometown. "You can't go home again," Isabel said, quoting F. Scott Fitzgerald. "Especially if they carted away your hometown in a dumpster." Isabel felt drained and transferred back to the 51 bus that would take her home. As she rode the bus, she thought of the lyrics to Joni Mitchell's song, "You don't know what you've got till it's gone...." Isabel couldn't wait to start driving away from all the memories just to be in a place that had no history or past for her. She felt like she could be the artist and paint whatever landscape, so to speak, for herself. At least she had to try, or she would regret it for the rest of her life.

A young man hopped on the bus talking loudly into his Bluetooth ear pods. Isabel sighed and prayed for patience as he continued to speak more loudly to be heard over the bus engines. She noticed the other passengers sighing, rolling their eyes, and looking wearily at the young man. He seemed oblivious. Isabel tried to catch his eye, but he was totally absorbed in his personal conversation, not so personal to everyone on the bus. She tried again, "Um, excuse me, but...."

He looked her square in the face and then, to her amazement, simply turned his back to her and spoke even more loudly into the Bluetooth. Isabel had assumed that she would not have to finish the sentence and that the rude behavior would stop. But instead, he looked straight at her and began to speak more loudly.

"Sorry, I didn't get that. Some chick was making noise!"

Isabel looked around at the other people on the bus, trying to catch an eye of support from anyone, but they either stared straight ahead or looked away. That made her even more furious, and her anger grew as her fists clenched. She was frightened at her thoughts of punching the guy in the face. But she took a deep breath and stopped herself. She had seen too many scenarios of road rage, mass shootings, and other irrational behavior, and she realized she might be the one with a smashed face.

But then, halfway back on the bus, she heard some faint singing. She looked back and saw two older women who looked like anyone's elementary school teacher with some mischief in their eyes. They became bolder and sang the immortal song, "The wheels on the bus go round, and round/round and round/round and round/the wheels on the bus go round and round/all through the town."

The infectious song known by everyone who had ever gone to school caught the man off guard, and he paused, but only for a second. Then he began to speak louder! The two women continued singing, and then three other people picked up the lyrics and began to sing it a bit louder. The singing became more vociferous, people's moods shifted, and their laughter sprinkled among the singing.

"The people on the bus go up and down, up, and down/up and down. The people on the bus go up and down all through the town." Isabel tentatively started singing too.

To Isabel's delight, she saw the face of the man speaking on his phone turn red, and he began to stammer and glance at all the people singing directly to him. By now, the whole bus was singing.

"Yeah, I don't know what's going on...some weirdos are singing..." the man stammered.

Suddenly the bus intercom burst to life, and the bus driver sang quite loudly. "The driver on the bus says move on back/move on back/move on back. The driver on the bus says, move on back/all through the town." Isabel laughed out loud and realized her thoughts of punching the guy were gone as she kept singing.

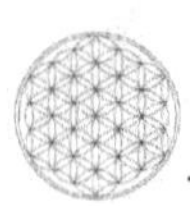

The now angry young man yanked fiercely on the exit cord and bellowed, "Hey! Hey! Let me out! Now!"

With the intercom still on, the entire bus heard the driver chuckle, "Absolutely! It will be my pleasure, sir!"

The bus driver expertly moved the bus to the curb, and the doors hissed open. The young man sprang from the exit door muttering into his Bluetooth, "I'll call you back...yeah, some real assholes on this bus!" As he settled on the sidewalk and the doors closed behind him, he flipped off the bus with both hands. The now united passengers broke out in cheers and laughter.

Isabel felt freedom and power in choosing to join the singing and witness the positive (and positively negative) results it created. It was such a small thing to do, but her heart was still singing, just remembering the moment's miracle. It felt good to choose a more positive direction than to focus on his bad behavior; it was empowering.

A few minutes later, the bus left Isabel on her block. She took a moment to watch it drive away as she relived the whole event. She concluded that it was amazing to see and experience whatever that was, and it was also weirdly magical.

Just then, the lyrics to a song her grandpa Bill used to sing to her years ago played in her mind. He sang this song to her many times, but she could only remember some of the lyrics.

Do you believe in magic..... in a young girl's heart? ......the music can free her whenever it starts. ... it's magic. If the music is ...., it makes you feel happy, like..... I'll tell you about the magic, and it'll free your soul.

Isabel blanked on many of the lyrics, but they touched her more profoundly now. Grandpa Bill always believed in the magic of music and often said, "I will just keep playing and singing till they take me off this planet!" And he did. Isabel thought he secretly wanted her to take up the mantle and become a musician, but it never took hold

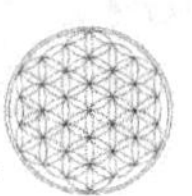

with her. She could never pick up an instrument and learn it nor sing in tune, but she did gain an appreciation of music spanning several eras and genres.

She pulled out her phone and sent an Instagram post:

Do You Believe in Magic?
Music is the Magic That Can Free Your Soul!

CHAPTER TWO

You Can't Always Get What You Want

Isabel was still feeling buoyant as she walked into her home. But as soon as she opened the door and smelled Chanel No. 5, the scent wrapped around her throat, causing her buoyancy to drop like a condemned prisoner through a trap door.

Her diminutive Grandma Anna was sitting in the living room with her parents, clutching the same oversized, pink leather Coach bag she's had for years. The old and venerable Coach bag was a family member in its own right. Anything you ever needed, Grandma Hotchkiss produced it from the shoulder bag, from a Band-Aid to needle and thread, ChapStick, scissors, mittens, pen, pencil, notepad, or mints. Isabel's mother once said, "If you opened the bag, you would see a tiny CVS store inside."

On seeing Isabel, she popped out of her chair with incredible speed considering her age (and the weight of her Coach bag). "Happy Birthday, Isabel!" Grandma was a contradiction of emotions. If there was any domestic tension or an actual argument in the air, she ignored it, the way she ignored just about anything that caused arguments and discord. And sure enough, she was smiling as if nothing was wrong, holding out a small rectangular gift-wrapped package.

"Thank you, Grandma Anna. I'm sure it's a wonderful present." Isabel was about to put the unopened gift in her pocket when she caught another look from her father; code to mean, *open the package now!* For her survival, Isabel unwrapped the package immediately. She recognized the robin's egg blue box from Tiffany's. She mentally sighed and was sure that Grandma Anna had gotten her the same gold necklace she had purchased for every Hotchkiss female family member dating back decades. And in her firm 1950s commitment to gender bias, males in the Hotchkiss family were given gold Tiffany rings engraved with the family crest.

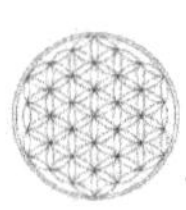

'*Note to self,*' thought Isabel. '*Explore the possibility of exchanging the ridiculous necklace for the Hotchkiss ring.*'

Ting. Isabel heard a text message alert. Her irritating brother, Benjamin, texted, **'*phony fake Izzy take a bow!*'**

Ting. **'*Shut up, you loser,*'** She shot back.

"Thank you, Grandma Anna. It's beautiful."

Ting' **'*Oh please, no presents unless they are expensive.*'**

Ting' **'*Idiot*'**

Texting was definitely a better way to fight with your brother in front of your parents. Izzy continued smiling.

Grandma left to go into the kitchen. Dad slipped in, "That is a much better attitude for all of us!"

The next moment Grandma Anna was coming into the dining room with a colossal éclair and one lit candle, singing, "*Happy Birthday to you, Happy Birthday to you, Happy Birthday dear Izzy, Happy Birthday to you!*"

"Your mother told me you said no birthday cakes, but you didn't say no birthday éclair." Grandma Anna was smiling, quite pleased that she had found a loophole in Isabel's request. With a great flourish, Grandma placed the birthday éclair in front of Isabel and looked expectantly at her. She added, "It's from Kornblatt's Deli, your favorite," as if that would help.

Inside, Isabel fumed but, simultaneously, was touched by the effort. She thought, '*What is it with loopholes and birthday cakes with this family?!*' So many thoughts and emotions to juggle confused her, and she was not prepared to blow out the candle as instructed by Grandma Anna.

In her hesitation, Benjamin grabbed it and said, "Here, let me," blowing out the candle. Isabel felt even angrier. Grandma Anna took out the candle, picked up the éclair, and handed it to Isabel. Isabel had barely said, "No thank you," before Benjamin tried to grab it again as he said, "I'll eat it." All three adults said simultaneously, "NO!"

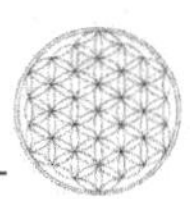

Grandma Anna sighed and shook her head. She took a deep breath and adjusted her posture to be at least an inch taller. She then spoke quite seriously as if she was proclaiming a profound observation, "You know, Isabel, there are children in North Korea who are starving and would consider this éclair a blessing."

"Really?" asked Isabel. "North Korean children starving? There are children starving all over the world. That is precisely the problem. This stupid éclair is not going to solve anything! Can you name any child that needs food? Name one!"

Benjamin gasped as his eyes went wide with disbelief. Even he knew that Isabel had taken it too far. He was too shocked even to send a text message to taunt her. He wanted to see how this would play out, so he kept his eyes wide open on everyone.

"Oh my," was all her grandma could muster while her eyebrows arched up like the yellow McDonald's arches.

Isabel's father did not usually tap into his anger, so his fury was unhinged and frightening. Phil growled, "You do not speak to my mother that way!" Suddenly Isabel knew that she had crossed a very consequential line. In her anger and frustration, she had not considered that Grandma Anna was, in fact, her dad's mother. And her son, Isabel's father, loved Grandma Anna very much.

When confronted with scary, out-of-control anger, some people flee or fold. Not

Isabel. She matched it with her indignity and fury. She doubled down, retorting, "It's a ridiculous statement. The concept of distributing eclairs to North Korean children is ...."

Phillip did something he had never done before; he grabbed Isabel by her shirt. It shocked them both. "JUST STOP, ISABEL!! For God's sake, stop!" Her father bellowed. The air froze into solid ice; time stopped. It was tragically evident that the whole family felt wounded by his action.

Her father's weary voice only slightly thawed the air. "I think we are all better off with you in your room," he said.

"I agree. Go back to your room," Isabel's mom said. She looked utterly defeated by the moods of her daughter.

Grandma just muttered, "Oh dear, oh dear."

As Isabel headed up the stairs, she found that her entire body drained itself of energy. She pulled herself up the stairs by grabbing onto the handrail.

Isabel sat on her bed and fought back the tears. Then she was angry that she had to fight back the tears. She slumped in her favorite chair and thought, '*What's the use?*' She thought about the album *Sour* by Olivia Rodrigo. Just like the album's theme, everything in Isabel's life had gone sour. No, not sour; bitter and dangerous.

Her best friend Ada had texted her earlier in the day to wish her a non-happy non-birthday. She was leaving for Morocco on a Peace Corps assignment in the morning, but Isabel desperately needed a mood booster from her friend. Ada was a rock star in Isabel's life. No matter what happened, she was there to make Isabel laugh.

Isabel texted, *'life sucks about right now'*

Ada: *'whatsup?'*

Isabel: *'just insulted my sweet Grandma... parents are none too happy*

Ada: *'shut up!!'*

Isabel: *'I'm a horrible person*

Ada: *'Well, Happy BD to you, girlfriend! You are doin it in style today! LOL'*

Isabel: *Turning 21 is hard*

Ada then sent a meme of a character from South Park hitting his head with this caption: *If you think turning 21 and becoming responsible for your actions is going to be fun, you're gonna have a bad time.*

Isabel: *Lmfao, I will miss you!*

Isabel went to her window, opened it, carefully stepped out on the narrow ledge, and shimmied onto the large Maple tree branch

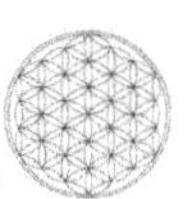

conveniently growing only a foot from the roof. She had used this escape route many times before, but now she just needed to sit. It gave her a moment to breathe and quiet the loud, angry voices in her head. She sat and gazed at the early evening sky.

To her surprise, her parents came out the front door and started talking in low monotones. But Isabel could hear them just fine when she leaned down a bit.

"What are we going to do with her? I feel like we have tried everything," her mom said. "It's ridiculous that she is so unhappy with her life or us! She has had such a privileged life compared to other kids."

Her father chimed in, "She reminds me of myself at her age, full of piss and vinegar they used to say. I thought I knew everything and saw the world in only black and white. Trust me, that simple view will change once she gets out in the world. Remember, out of chaos and pain comes revelation."

"I think she has been in the chaos and pain phase far too long. She is just at war with herself but hasn't figured that one out yet. Her being gone will be a good thing for the entire family, and I am ready for the peace it will bring," her mother added.

Isabel was devastated and did not want to hear anymore. She turned and silently climbed in through her window. Slumped in her chair, utterly defeated, Isabel admitted her life was in a privileged, safe bubble in the universe. She remembered reading an Opinion Column in the New York Times in which the author wondered if the world had simply given up on decency and could not get along. The writer had called it 'existential angst.' She had to look up what existential angst meant, and before she finished the article, she found herself nodding, wiping away tears before they fell and officially became weeping.

"Existential angst not only derives from the human inability to think, feel, and act in the world or experience a love for life, but also from the fear of the possibility of nonexistence and death."

Isabel knew she needed something that could help her discover how to get out of her recently discovered existential angst. She felt an incredible emptiness inside and a desire to fill that hole with answers. Silently she acknowledged that her personality was becoming more threatening and impossible to be around as time went on.

Isabel's eye caught the well-thumbed volume of *Harry Potter and The Sorcerer's Stone* on her bookshelf. She loved the world of Harry Potter and its transformations through magic, spells, and alchemy. She pulled down the book and held it close to her heart. Reading it had brought so much happiness to her life. The author of *Harry Potter* had written about a world inclusive of many creatures; straight, gay, ghosts (gay ghosts), witches, imps, and giants. The book helped Isabel proudly accept her entourage of assorted friends unconditionally.

She opened the book, and a forgotten piece of paper fell out.

What do alchemists do?

Alchemist: Someone Who **Transforms Things for the Better**

Years ago, Isabel remembered reading that J.K. Rowling wanted to become an alchemist, so not knowing what that meant, she did a search. Now, Isabel fantasized for a moment about becoming an alchemist, too, and how she would be able to wave a magic wand or cast a spell to take away all the injustices, hatred, dishonesty, and greed to make the world a better place to live.

Isabel then had an uncomfortable feeling that everything would not turn out like the *Harry Potter*, *Star Wars*, or *Lord of the Rings* novels she loved. The power had shifted to the world's Voldemorts, Saurons, and Darth Vaders. She imagined that there was a good chance, the way the world was going, that evil black magic would prevail, and the good guys might lose, or at best, the good guys would settle for a pretty crappy, fear-filled existence alongside the bad guys.

Isabel had never felt this way before. So much in the world seemed beyond repair. In the past, she had always been able to figure out what was wrong and what to do to make it right. But now, everything seemed uncertain, and she felt helpless. It seemed that evil and negativity were

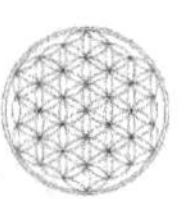

stalking the world, cackling evilly, setting up house in her brain, giving her choices to redecorate in only grays, blacks, and swirling fog.

She snapped back into reality and remembered the words her parents had spoken. They stung, not because they were inaccurate, but maybe because they were true. Isabel decided right then and there to grab a few extra things and leave for her trip earlier than planned. *'That's it,'* she thought, *'I'm out of here.'* She slipped the book back into the bookshelf and grabbed her jacket.

She shoved her cell phone, charger, savings, wallet, and a few books into her backpack and stormed downstairs, ready to make a dramatic exit. Only silence met her. The house was empty. To add insult to injury, they had all left to go to dinner without her. She suddenly felt very alone, but it only fortified her decision to leave. *'They want me gone; they even said it. They will finally be happy when I leave,'* Isabel thought.

She opened the refrigerator to grab the éclair for her road trip. The plate sat there just as lonely as she felt, with a few crumbs and a note from her brother. 'You didn't want it, so I ate it. Everyone thinks you're an idiot.' B. The message made her furious. She didn't think her family actually took a vote, and there was a unanimous agreement that she was an idiot, but she did feel they were not happy with her behavior.

She left a note for her parents. 'I am leaving for my trip early, so you will get the peace you want. I will be going offline for my own peace and sanity. Love, Isabel.' She debated on the "Love," but Isabel was, if anything, good-hearted, and yes, she did love them even though they were completely wrong about her and everything else. Yes, it was a bit dramatic, but Isabel knew she needed the break; she needed a break from her mind, her feelings, her life, her family, and the world.

She quietly hustled over the lawn to enter the workshop/garage and opened the wooden barn-like door. "Hey, Van Go," she greeted her beloved van.

Looking at the outside of the van, which she painted in her interpretation of *"Starry Night,"* merging into his painting of *"Crows over Wheat Fields,"* fortified her resolve to start her journey. She felt a lot of satisfaction because she had prepared for her trip long before all this family miscommunication. She had also painted the ceiling inside the van with the *"Starry Night"* painting. She was nervous about the liberty she took in painting it with DayGlo paint. Even more so was the fact that she added a few more stars vibrating in that miraculous universe.

Isabel had always been fascinated with the artist Van Gogh and felt his face was filled with such feelings of confusion, longing, and loneliness. She took particular satisfaction with the fact that she and the artist both had red hair and blue eyes, the rarest physical combination in the world. Only 7% of the world's population had that combo. She had also discovered that red hair resulted from a broken chromosome in the MC1R gene, which according to her friend, Mikey Schlotzsky, a chemistry nerd, made her an "official, scientific mutant." She wondered if that had anything to do with her chronic depression. She thought 21 was when Van Gogh started exhibiting signs of mental illness. She seemed to remember he was always looking for something in himself but never found it. It did give her pause, but she had to keep moving before she lost her confidence.

Her first destination was the 73rd annual Lummi Nation Stommish Water Festival in Bellingham, Washington, on the Lummi reservation. The tribe had a celebration planned for the send-off of a 5000-pound, 25-foot-high totem pole to Washington, D.C. This pilgrimage was going to symbolize many causes that concern the tribe and other Indian communities nationwide.

Her gauges read that she had 20% battery power, to her dismay. Isabel estimated that gave her only 90 miles of energy stored in the battery. That would not get her anywhere near Bellingham just on the electric charge. She could use the gasoline tank, but Isabel's goal was to use the electric charge as much as possible.

But then she remembered that the Walmart in Wood City next to the adorably named Troutdale was one of those Super Walmarts

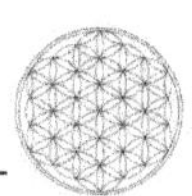

that welcomed R.V.s, campers, and anybody who needed to stay for a night or two. They also had electric charging stations. She knew that she could spend the night there for free and, at the same time, recharge Van Go's battery.

When she arrived at Walmart, her sense of independence and self-reliance gave way to grumpy frustration when she saw the long line waiting at the dozen or so battery charging stations. Several were R.V.s. *'When did they start making electric R.V.s?'* she thought. Then she remembered that Winnebagos and other monster R.V.s recharged their electric battery to power the self-indulgent wide-screen televisions, cappuccino makers, and kitchen appliances the same way an electric car would charge itself.

As Isabel drove into the Walmart parking lot, all she could think of were her parent's unending negative comments about gas-guzzling R.V.s when she saw a massive R.V. in the electric charging zone with a Prius in tow. The Prius was getting the charge.

Isabel noticed a man sitting next to the R.V. with the Prius. He had a grizzly white beard and was very contentedly sipping a lager. His feet were propped up on a large, plastic, blue igloo cooler which she estimated contained at least two dozen more beers. He wore a T-shirt stretched over a generous belly that Isabel concluded was the dedicated reward of a lifetime of beer. The shirt read: *Semper Fi, The Few, The Proud, The Marines.* The graphic was a multicolored, extremely annoyed screaming eagle with massive black talons clutching a banner that redundantly read, *"Semper Fidelis."*

The man watched the charcoal embers glow in a Hibachi on the paved parking lot. Isabel felt that he was almost a parody of the type of person who'd be driving a massive R.V. and probably had political leanings diametrically opposed to anyone she'd typically associate with. But just as she thought this, the man did quite an unusual thing. He broke into a large sunburst of a smile and waved directly at her. Isabel found herself waving back.

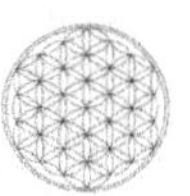

With some struggle, the man extricated himself from his low beach chair. Red-faced and breathing heavily, the man trundled over to her. Isabel began to regret her involuntary friendliness.

'Oh, God, now I have to be nice to MAGA hat,' she thought. In reality, his bald head was hatless, but other signs led her to assume he was one.

Isabel muttered, "I don't want to be nice; I want to be left alone."

She decided to wave and slowly drive off, but a blasting horn behind her made her realize that a massive Ford F-350 was blocking her escape route. *'When did pickup trucks start being designed by Megatron?'* she thought. She couldn't drive off, no matter how annoyed she felt at the moment, so she pulled next to the Prius. Then she slid open the glass window after unlocking it (the original Metro did not have car windows but a utilitarian, clear sliding plastic window arrangement). Smiling thinly, hoping the man got the message that she didn't want to have any conversations that were sure to start with, "What's a young woman like you driving a van like this?"

While taking in Isabel's vehicle, the man smiled and nodded like he was visiting a place he had long ago left. "That's a '55 Harvester International Metro Van, isn't it?" asked the man.

Isabel was caught off guard, "Yes! But how'd you know?"

He just kept talking, "The '55 was the last model with that four-bolt bumper and split windshield. Beautiful rig. Did you know the designer genius Raymond Loewy designed the Metro? He was called "The Man Who Shaped America" and "The Father of Industrial Design." He designed some of the most beautiful cars and the most snap dazzle steam engines and locomotives in history."

"Um, no. I did not know that...."

Before Isabel could say more, "You're far too young to remember people who had the job I did. Ancient history, but back in the day, I was a milkman." He continued, "I drove for the Alpenrose Dairy in Portland in a truck like this one."

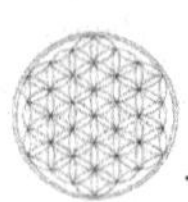

"Of course, I've heard of your job and the Alpenrose Dairy. This was one of their trucks," Isabel proudly shared. She felt her voice had a rather smug attitude in her response to the friendly man, even though judging from that land yacht he was driving, he was probably a destroyer of the environment. She was sure he was of the generation that had caused most of the world's problems, including climate change.

Isabel added, "I played softball at Alpenrose Dairy when I was younger and raced at the quarter midget track."

"My!" the man grinned. "Seems like you spent more time there than I did."

Isabel's heart softened, "Look, I'm sorry about how I answered your question about my van. I was kind of obnoxious." She sincerely did not want to have her crappy mood infect any more people.

The man waved her apology off. "Actually, I deserved it with you driving up in the same rig I used to drive. I try not to assume anybody knows anything. You know what happens if you assume something, don't you?"

"No, I don't," stated Isabel.

"To assume makes an ASS out of U and M.E.!" The man obviously delighted in that old quote and laughed out loud.

Isabel thought for a moment and realized what he said was a little too close to home as she was the one doing that same thing a few minutes earlier. It made her slightly uncomfortable and curious about how this interaction would unfold.

"That sounds like something my dad would say."

He cocked his head like he was listening for something. "That's an awfully quiet engine for a Metro. Wait, is it off?"

"No, it's electric," Isabel said.

"Electric?! In a '55 Metro Van?! Well, slap me silly and call me stupid!"

"My mom converted it from the inline six it originally had. She's an electrical engineer," said Isabel. She half expected him to blurt

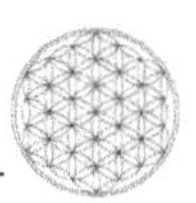

out something negative about women being mechanics and electrical engineers. But instead, he nodded appreciatively and smiled.

"Excellent," he said. He took a step back to look at *"Starry Night"* on the side of the van. He paused and said, "Let me guess, you named the van, Van Gogh?!"

"Exactly!" Isabel tried to hide her surprise from him and added, "I only named him Van Go, G-O, like go."

"Sure, I get it. Very clever, very clever!" He held out his hand and said, "By the way, I'm Hank. Hank Cooper." He went on, "I'm not that educated in art history. But do you know the song, *Vincent,* by Don McLean?"

"Starry, Starry Night?" Isabel asked.

"Yeah. When I first heard it, it blew me away! Of course, McLean went down a few pegs in my estimation when I heard *American Pie.* I know he meant it as honest criticism of where society was headed back then. Everybody was right pissed at the government. Most were as crooked as a barrel of fishhooks, entangled by a tornado of lies, especially Tricky Dick Nixon," Hank explained.

"Seems like not much has changed," Isabel mused.

"Aye, sadly, that appears to be the truth. I never thought anybody could make Nixon would look good!" Hank smiled and added, "But I don't believe anyone thinks rock n' roll ended with Buddy Holly and Ritchie Valens. No, siree, the Beatles and the Stones had something to say about that. So did Led Zeppelin, Springsteen, and Elvis Costello."

Isabel opened her door, reached out her hand, and said, "Isabel Hotchkiss."

"Why, that is a beautiful name, almost Victorian."

Isabel explained, "Yes, it goes back to the early 1800s. I think it was some ancestor of mine who was named Hotchkiss. She founded a private school which I believe is still in existence."

Hank looked at the stars before saying, "You should find out more about her. My family considers ancestors very important; we consult them all the time. So, Isabel Hotchkiss, do you think you could let me take a look at the inside of your van?"

Hank realized why Isabel was hesitating and blurted out, "Oh, just a second." He called out to the open window of his R.V., "Roxanne. Roxanne? Would you come out here for a moment?"

Roxanne yelled, "Just a second, Hank, I'm putting away the dinner dishes."

Hank blushed, "Oops! That was my job!"

With a tinge of sarcasm, Isabel heard the same voice say, "Yes, it was, dearest."

Isabel felt foolish for not trusting these two older people as she stepped down on the pavement. Isabel tried to speak up not to inconvenience Roxanne, but Hank would have nothing of it. He shook his head and pointed his finger at Isabel before taking command of the situation. "I insist. I'd want my daughter and granddaughter to be as cautious as you are. I can tell you can handle yourself, but unfortunately, there are a lot of bad actors out there in the world. I call them Bad Actors on a Bad Day in Bedrock!"

Roxanne came down the steps of the R.V. and said, "Okay, Hank, dearest, what is it?" Then she took in Isabel and the van and smiled wide.

She was a handsome, slightly stocky woman whose straight, and silver/steel gray hair fell to her waist. Two simple tortoiseshell hair clips kept it from falling into her face. She was the kind of person who would look at home in a garden wearing overalls, which she was wearing. Isabel immediately liked her.

"Ah, well, I can understand your excitement, Hank," Roxanne nodded towards Van Go, "and she looks about the same age as Cecilia."

"That's our granddaughter," Hank said to Isabel. "Roxanne, this is Isabel Hotchkiss. She wouldn't let me see the inside of her van unless a chaperone accompanied me."

"Good for her. I wouldn't let a beer-guzzling old man into my van with that grubby, ridiculous right-wing, macho T-shirt on either, "said Roxanne.

"Hey, now! I love this T-shirt. Wouldn't go into Walmart without it."

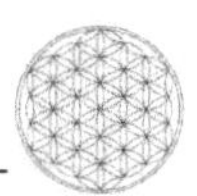

"And I won't go anywhere in public with you if you're wearing it." Roxanne added, "Even in this Walmart parking lot, it's embarrassing."

Isabel laughed and then realized she hadn't laughed in a while. She was eager to show Hank and Roxanne the interior of Van Go, "Stand right here in the doorway. I want you to get the full effect when I close the door."

Once inside, Isabel turned off the regular light and switched on a black light. The ceiling glowed and exploded into a riot of swirling colors. Isabel was delighted at their unison, "Oh, my!" "Holy cow!" when taking in the blacklight DayGlo version of *Starry Night*.

Isabel asked, "Do you think Van Gogh would mind that I painted Starry Night using DayGlo colors?"

"Naw, I believe he would consider it pure brilliance. After all, his art is living on, and you are helping to keep his legend and memory alive. And I like it better than the Immersion Art Exhibit we just saw!"

"But so many critics said it was fantastic," said Isabel.

"Yeah, well, when I was in there, all the music, swelling, exploding visions, moving visions, and painting visions were a bit overwhelming. I bristled because it felt like somebody else was telling me what to look at and what was important about Van Gogh and his paintings. I will decide what's important for me. I don't need wall-sized and ceiling-sized projections and music selected for me."

"Well, I rather enjoyed it," Roxanne added.

"My parents took us to New York when I was 16," said Isabel. "One of the first places we stopped was The Museum of Modern Art, and I saw *Starry Night*. Seeing the actual painting; changed something in me."

"And that inspired you to paint the van?" asked Roxanne.

"Yes, but it took me a long time to get the courage to paint the van. I even asked a self-portrait of Van Gogh for permission, "Isabel confessed.

"Did he give it?" asked Roxanne.

"Not right away. I don't think," Isabel said.

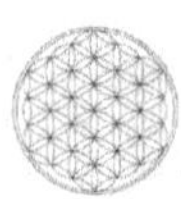

"By the way, I wonder which one you asked," said Hank.

"What do you mean? asked Isabel

"Well, Van Gogh painted at least 35 self-portraits," Hank said.

"35? I knew of a few, but I didn't know there were that many!" Isabel exclaimed.

Hank laughed. "They found another self-portrait behind the painting, *The Potato Eaters*. Could it be that you didn't hear anything because you requested permission from the wrong self-portrait?"

Roxanne swatted his shoulder. "Oh, Hank! Stop it!" She turned to Isabel and said, "I apologize for his obnoxious sense of humor. You are not obligated to laugh either."

"Or, maybe he had his bad ear towards you?!" Hank added.

Isabel laughed. "Yea, that's pretty good. And I'm used to it. It's the same kind of groaners my dad comes up with, and my just mom rolls her eyes."

At the thought of her parents, Isabel had a slight pang of regret about how she left so abruptly. Then a thought crossed Isabel's mind, and she laughed out loud.

"What's so funny?" asked Hank.

"Well, I just thought about Van Gogh's self-portraits."

"And?" said Hank.

"Well, he was a guy who painted pictures of himself a lot. If he were alive today, he probably would have taken 43 million selfies," Isabel said.

Hank and Roxanne laughed out loud.

"Oh God, Hank, she's no better than you are. I won't come to your defense anymore, Isabel; you deserve each other."

"But in all seriousness," said Isabel, "When I saw *Starry Night* at the Museum, that's when I truly fell in love with his art. While I looked at the original painting before me, I felt there was no separation between seeing his art and experiencing his vision pouring onto a blank white space. I sensed his courage to use that thick paint of swirling colors. I could see the grooves, the furrows of his brush strokes put there in

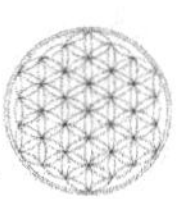

the painting. I felt he was there, cosmically, quantumly, if that's a word, that he was there with me."

Roxanne sighed, "Oh, dear, that's beautiful. And your van is beautiful."

"I'll bet, Isabel, you've reached your own opinion about that aircraft carrier we're driving!" Hank said as they all took a seat by the RV.

"Oh, stop being a tease, Hank. I swear you just look for an argument," Roxanne interrupted.

"I had some negative thoughts about it, to be honest," said Isabel.

"I'll be the first to admit, it's pretty embarrassing," said Roxanne. She continued, "Two old fogeys, who are members of Greenpeace, Sierra Club, and Earth First! driving that land yacht."

"Wait! Shut Up!" Isabel blurted out. "What possessed you to buy the R.V. then?"

Isabel saw Hank's face soften, his eyes tearing up before he said.

"We didn't. It belonged to my kid brother, Jimmy. He passed away from COVID...about..wow, it's been over a year now." Hank wiped his eyes, and Roxanne hugged his arm. "We kidded Jimmy a lot for buying it. He thought it would be the perfect joke to bequeath it to us. He was right. Keeping it seemed like the right thing to do, for now. It gives me fond memories of him anyway."

Roxanne added, "Both Hank and Jimmy have/had a wicked sense of humor. Hank wanted to put some decals for each ecological organization on the back of the R.V. just to mess with people's heads, but I reminded him that some of the members of those groups would take it as an R.V. owner flipping them the bird. These days a lot of people have lost their sense of humor."

"But nothing funny about how masterfully human beings have successfully destroyed much of the planet. It seems that most decisions are made for short-term financial gain without considering the long-term effects on the planet, the ecosystem, our water systems, communities, small businesses, our health, and need I go on?" Isabel spewed out. Then she added, "I'm sorry, I seem to be a doomer, and I often yell about unjust things. My mom said I was at war with myself; maybe that is the problem."

Hank replied, "Well, I'm just a boomer, not a doomer." They laughed and then sat contentedly looking at the ebbing flames of the Hibachi.

"Roxanne and I used to teach martial arts to inner-city kids," said Hank.

"The most rewarding part was teaching them how to navigate life and deal with their inner and outer struggles," said Roxanne.

"Do you know who Bruce Lee was?" asked Hank.

"I... I think so. Wasn't he the movie star and kung fu actor?"

"Yes, he was, but he was more than that. He was a true master and philosopher."

"He had a unique way of looking at the world that has helped us stay fairly balanced over the years. One of our favorite quotes he said was, *Be Like Water, My Friend. Empty our minds, be formless, shapeless, like water. You put water into a cup; it becomes the cup. You put water in a bottle; it becomes the bottle. You put water in a teapot; it becomes a teapot. Water can flow, or it can crash. Be like water, my friend.*"

"That's really beautiful," said Isabel.

"It is," said Roxanne. "And it is also very, very hard to achieve. It takes most people a lifetime to achieve such acceptance of what life throws at them."

Isabel silently acknowledged how she often bitterly questioned how life kept throwing bean bags at her head. She wondered if she could ever achieve what Bruce Lee counseled.

And with that, Hank and Roxanne started to pick up and prepare for bed. Isabel said, "I better call it a night too. I've got to buy tires and have a lot of driving to do in the morning. But I can't tell you how much I enjoyed this. It's really been special for me, thank you."

Roxanne hugged Isabel and said, "You take care, Isabel. And good luck on your journey. I hope you find what you're looking for."

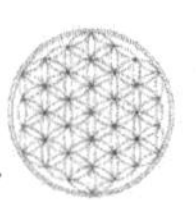

"Or what's looking for you finds you," said Hank.

As Isabel lay there thinking about the day's events, she watched the *Be Like Water* Bruce Lee video a few times and thought about how she resisted most things. She even resisted meeting these two wonderful human beings. The realization that she fought against most of the changes in her life was eye-opening. She wondered what it would be like to be more open and flexible.

As she switched her phone to her playlist, the song from the Rolling Stones played, *You Can't Always Get What You Want.* As she listened to the lyrics, she laughed out loud at how appropriate they were for her. Today was just what she needed, but it certainly was not what she had planned or wanted. Isabel was surprised at how contented she felt. She was inspired to pull out her phone and send an Instagram post.

Sage Advice from me and Bruce Lee:
Be Like Water, My Friend

CHAPTER THREE

The Resilient Human Spirit

The following day, Isabel got up very early. She was surprised that Hank and Roxanne had left even earlier. Unbeknownst to her, Hank later unplugged his Prius and gave her van the plug to fully charge it before morning. She noticed an envelope taped to her driver's side window. Opening it, she saw that inside was a CD and a note.

Dear Isabel,

It was so lovely meeting you. You give us hope that the younger generation is still searching for answers. Just the search itself will uncover many truths for you. But don't forget to enjoy the journey along the way, which is often more important than the destination.

BTW- You mentioned you needed tires for Van Go. I highly recommend you go to Walmart; great prices and the best selection. I suggest the all-season Wranglers 235/75R17.5. It's what I put on the barge, and I think they would work well on the old Alpenrose Dairy truck.

Underneath were Hank and Roxanne's cell phone numbers.

Isabel smiled and taped the card onto her dashboard. Before doing so, she carefully divided the card to see the image and the note inside. The card was a picture of Vincent van Gogh's *Starry Night*.

Thankfully Walmart opened very early so she could follow Hank's advice before heading out of town. She was relieved when she noticed that her battery was fully charged, thanks to Hank and Roxanne. She picked up a few more provisions for her trip and turned to say goodbye to Portland. Being alone in a Walmart parking lot was not how she envisioned her send-off, but she was determined not to let it bring her mood down.

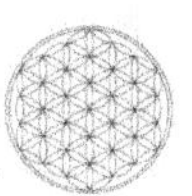

"Be like water," she said. "Accept and flow into what is going on around you." Isabel sat still for a moment. She took a deep breath and surprisingly felt calmer. "Be like water," she said again and then began to laugh because she heard Hank's voice say, "Be like water... in other words, don't forget to hydrate your brain." Then she imagined Roxanne swatting him and giving him an exasperated look. "Hank! I swear to God!"

Once settled back in the van, Isabel drove up Interstate 5 toward the Lummi reservation. It was 20 miles from the Canadian border and only about 200 miles away. Even though she was a few days ahead of schedule, the festival was officially starting today, so there was no need to make any detours along the way.

As she drove, the Cascade snow-covered Mountain Range appeared on her van's west side as a traveling companion through the Columbia Gorge. Mount Hood was the mountain God that watched over Portland. Despite its majesty, she thought that the Cascade Range looked like the logo for Paramount Pictures from a certain angle. Its beauty made her smile today as she began her long drive.

Isabel popped in the CD to listen to the story of Van Gogh's Starry Night; she felt like she was creating a total immersion experience with the card staring at her, her van painted on the inside and outside, and now the fascinating story behind it all. It made her chuckle, and she wished she could share this moment with her new friend, Hank. She felt sure he might like this experience better!

Narrator:
There is universal agreement that Van Gogh was a tortured soul who tragically ended his life before he gained notoriety. But few know that he was also a very passionate and empathetic individual that created over 2000 works of art.

He didn't start painting until he was twenty-seven years old and died just ten years later from a self-inflicted gunshot wound which became infected.

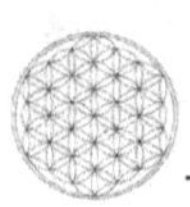

But thankfully most of his art survives and continues to inspire countless people to abandon themselves into the beauty and passion of his brushstrokes.

Starry Night depicts Van Gogh's view from his east-facing window, just before sunrise, in the asylum, Saint Remy De Provence. The asylum was a former monastery, and Van Gogh's first painting was in June of the year 1889. He painted that view 21 times. The room had iron bars; sometimes, he would include the iron bars in his painting, and sometimes he didn't. The Village depicted in the paintings is imaginary. The cypress tree may be interpreted as a symbol of death and mourning because cypress trees are often planted in cemeteries. Van Gogh thought the impressionistic painting was a failure as he wrote to many, including his beloved brother, Theo. Van Gogh thought, *'the stars were too big.'* Many art critics believe that the painting and the letters he wrote expressed a deep desire to find religious and spiritual comfort in the celestial images he created.

The narrator went on to say that Van Gogh struggled to find his place in the world. One interesting fact that few people know is that he was largely self-taught and highly intelligent. Some people think Van Gogh's creations at the asylum were influenced by mental illness. Ironically, isolation was good for him, and Van Gogh created some of his most famous paintings and beloved art pieces while in mental asylums. Fortunately, Saint Remy De Provence was a progressive institution that embraced music and art as forms of therapy and felt that nature was good for people. However, it was not enough to cure Van Gogh of whatever mental illness he suffered through. Many speculated that his mental illness was bipolar disorder because his moods were erratic. Thankfully Van Gogh's artistic genius had an outlet, and he was much better when given the time to create and paint. But if mental illness is not adequately treated, it only worsens over time, and Van Gogh's precarious mental state was no exception.

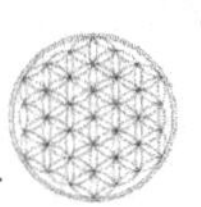

Isabel listened to the whole thing and found herself halfway to her destination for the night by the time she finished it. She had chosen the Lummi reservation for several reasons. They had a Harvest Festival, and at the same time, they had Indian recognition day. But even more fascinating to Isabel was that the Lummi Tribe had carved and was sending a special totem pole to Washington, D.C., to highlight their belief in Native American reparations. It was also to make a statement about the unfair treatment of all American Indians by the U.S. Government concerning all the broken treaties in the past centuries to a Sovereign Nation.

As she got closer to the reservation, she noticed more and more totem poles ranging from carved, unpainted, left to fight the elements to colorful, magnificent pieces of art. She particularly loved the ones with glorious, proud thunderbirds and other shamanic, sacred animals—most depicted sacred tribal celebrations through which their ancestors were etched to perpetually watch over future generations.

It seemed that other people had the same idea as she did, as there was quite a line waiting to get into the parking area for the festival. She found a parking spot and strolled towards the entrance with just a little searching. She paid her $15.00 admission fee and walked in. There was much excitement and activity, with many tribal members walking around in ceremonial costumes. She felt a pang of guilt thinking of them as costumes because they had so much history, symbolism, and meaning to the person wearing them.

A small billboard-like sign caught her attention; at least three dozen pictures of women and girls were on it. It was a ragtag collection of photographs, all of them female. As far as Isabel could tell, they ranged in age from around 9 to 35, maybe older. Some photos were formal portraits from high school yearbooks, Proms, and Sears. The others were informal home photos, some in color and some in black and white. Isabel read the words above them, *In Honor and Sacred Memory of the disappeared, missing, or murdered women and girls of our Lummi family 2000-2021. May the Great Spirit gather these stolen treasures and bring them and any grieving family comfort.*

Isabel knew enough not to be surprised about injustices on the reservation. She'd read about the alcohol problems, drug abuse, and violence against Native American women. But she was still overwhelmed with sadness at the pictures of the victims. Most were smiling, completely unaware of the tragedy that would befall them. She knew that many people didn't know, didn't care, or were preoccupied with their lives during these tumultuous times. They couldn't take the time to care about what happened to these human beings who had so much stolen from them. Throughout history, some people took their land, some took away their tribe's dignity, some even took lives, and most just looked on with an air of indifference.

Isabel also knew about the Christian conversion schools and how many children had been torn away from their parents, their tribe, their families, and everything they knew and trusted. They were forced to attend white schools while stripped of their culture and punished for speaking their native languages. And now, she thought, even today, they are being systematically discriminated against in death.

Isabel knew all this, but she did not know why there was a tiny red dress fluttering in the wind, hanging from the billboard, or what it represented. It looked so innocent, so forlorn, and so unprotected. She found herself weeping uncontrollably, and then she felt guilty. Yes, she was crying for them, but also for herself. It was, she felt, so selfish and self-centered of her. Those faces staring back at her were women who most likely met a terrible, horrible fate, alone and terrified. She knew her frustration and anger were nothing compared to those victims, their parents, families, and tribe, and how they all suffered! She could not stop weeping.

Then she felt the presence of someone, no, several people close to her. She felt a hand on her shoulder. A soft, gentle female voice said, "Thank you for mourning our lost sisters. I'm sure their spirits are comforted by your caring."

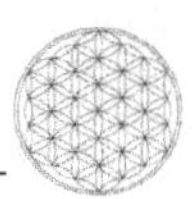

Isabel turned around and saw three women standing close, forming a wall between her and the rest of the festival. Two were dressed in ceremonial garb, soft Buckskin skirts beautifully embroidered and celebrated by feathers and colorful beadwork. The other woman wore clothes that could only be described as "cowgirl ready" barrel riding, steer riding, lassoing, blue jeans, and a cowboy hat. The two women in ceremonial garb looked about the same age as her mom. The cowgirl smiled ruefully and said, "You know, it's OK to cry for yourself as well. We are all sisters, and we are all women." The women all smiled and nodded. Isabel felt protected and cared for and somewhat ashamed because, yes, she was crying for herself as well as the victims.

"I'm sorry, but I feel embarrassed for crying for myself. My mom calls my problems first-world problems," said Isabel.

"Oh, you mean white people's problems?" said one of the women. The women all laughed. Isabel felt her face turn completely crimson.

"I don't think anybody deserves to be happy, especially me, because the whole world feels so messed up," Isabel said.

"Yes, it is messed up. We can plan and work for our dreams and goals, and yet along the way, the world can break our hearts many times," said one of the women dressed in traditional garb. She held out her hand. "My name is Rosemary."

The other two women held out their hands. "Anna."

"Maureen."

"Hello, my name is Isabel. I understand the whole billboard except for the red dress. What is the symbolism of this?"

A cloud fell over the women's faces. Rosemary said, "The red dresses symbolize all the women and girls missing or murdered. They represent the epidemic of violence against Indigenous women, and it has been going on for years."

"For decades," said Anna. "And ignored for decades, till now, we hope."

"But red dresses? Is that a kind of symbolism to your tribe?" asked Isabel.

Anna replied, "No, not when it first started. Jaimie Black, a Metis artist, saw them in Bogota, Colombia, where 40 women in the town square wore them to protest and demand answers about what happened to their 'disappeared' men and women. An unknown but brave woman climbed on top of a statue in the square wearing a red dress, and she called out to the crowd, "Donde Estan?! Donde Estan?!" "Where are they?" And the crowd picked up the chant. It became the chant of the disappeared. "Where are they?"

Maureen added, "It inspired Jaimie to create The REDress Project in 2010 to bring awareness to the disproportionate number of missing and murdered indigenous women."

"We needed to bring that energy home to our people to ask the same question and demand answers from our federal government, state officials, and local police departments. Homicide is the third leading cause of death among indigenous women ages 10-24, and native women are victims of murder more than ten times the national average," said Rosemary.

Isabel stopped walking and stood there with her mouth open, unsure what to say.

Maureen linked arms with Isabel and said, "Let's walk." Isabel willingly took Maureen's arm, and after a few yards, Isabel began smelling the most delicious aroma; a cross between waffles, pancakes, and French fries.

"What is that wonderful smell?" Isabel asked.

Anna chuckled and said, "A simple comfort food, but with a complicated past."

"Kind of like us!" Rosemary said.

They ended up in front of a booth displaying signage, "*Fry bread - $1.00 - just like your mama still makes.*" They grabbed a hot slab of delicious fry bread to nibble on while Maureen guided Isabel.

"Now let me show you the main attraction!" She gently guided Isabel to a tent in the middle of the festival to view the massive totem pole.

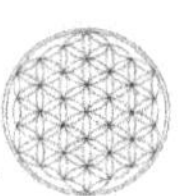

"It was carved by members of the House of Tears from our tribe. It will be making many stops along the way. We hope this gets the attention of the president and Congress in D.C. We call it, *The Red Road to D.C. Totem Pole to Protect Sacred Sites*. She leaned in and added, "Indians tend to over-explain things, so the government understands!" They all laughed.

She pointed out various symbols on the totem pole. "The red handprint, usually painted across the mouth, symbolizes the silence forced upon us by threats and violence. It is also a symbol of solidarity to those of our sisters who are still missing and, in most cases, murdered and whose voices have been forever silenced."

She continued, "The raindrops carved into the pole look like tears. All tears are water, and as such, they also bring attention to the terrible state of the rivers and waterways of our country. Like in nature, one thing flows into the other: the endangered fish, including the sacred salmon. The sacred salmon represents us, The Salmon People, and our survival. We don't think of these as Indian or tribal issues; they are everyone's issues. This totem pole is to open eyes and hearts with the art and bring awareness to these issues that will affect all human beings."

Isabel was staring transfixed at the totem pole. She was fascinated by the intricate carvings that carried so much meaning. She always appreciated how powerful the arts were and being around other like-minded people felt comforting. The Lummi people were known for their incredible artistic abilities, prolifically expressed throughout their weavings, carvings, and beadwork.

They were not far from the entrance to the festival and heard some loud commotion that did not seem to go with the fun-filled festivities. When they investigated, they saw a line of pickup trucks full of angry men and women taunting, "This land is our land" and "Read the memo. America's not yours anymore!" Signs read, *We won. You lost. Get over it!* and *Winners can break treaties!*

People at the festival were very uncomfortable and increasingly scared. To make matters worse, the mob was drinking, which made them feel very bold and uninhibited. Several of them started to walk toward the festival group continuing their ugly chants. She noted the worried looks on the faces of the people around her. It was more real than watching the riots in downtown Portland on television and smelling the tear gas and the smoke from the burning fires on the street a few miles from her home. It was coming toward her, and it wasn't miles away, but minutes away, and they meant people harm.

Then she heard the sound of drums and the hard, tonal chanting of the Lummi women singing their tribal songs. Firm and insistent singing. They silently formed an impenetrable line, beating drums powerfully and heading directly toward the angry mob. It was a sight to behold as they were all dressed in red dresses and had a look of determination and focus that was hard to match. Isabel saw the mob take stock of the women coming like a tide emerging from the earth, determined and powerful. Even from this distance, she could see the men and women's faces recalibrating.

The angry mob stopped in their tracks and looked at each other with an expression of, "What the hell do we do now?" If it were not such a dangerous and dramatic situation, Isabel would have nervously giggled. The protestors and women of the tribes were in a standoff with each other, and no one moved. The red dresses looked to Isabel like the flames of a wildfire. The women's chanting grew louder; they were steadfast in their drumming and singing. Isabel could see the sweat appearing on the men's brows. Something had to give, something to shake things up to deescalate their fury and rage.

Isabel jumped into action. She made a beeline for Van Go, thankfully parked relatively close to the entrance. As she was expertly maneuvering the van back toward the potential riot, she hoped things would not escalate. She could see their hate-filled faces and fingers pointing at the Lummi women while spewing spittle and curses. It immediately occurred to her that she would block the

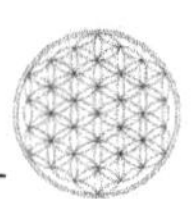

intersection directly in front of the angry protesters on the right. It also occurred to her that in a matter of moments, her van would be surrounded by them.

BLAAAAAAAAATTTTTT!!! The sound of Isabel pulling on the unbelievably loud air horn shattered the air just as she had hoped. It sent the mob of men and women scattering back to their vehicles with panicked expressions. And just as she wagered, the Lummi Indian women were so intensely focused on their defiance of those protestors that the horn didn't even shake them. In fact, they seemed to be swept up by the horn; the blast made them rise up and deliver their blood-curdling warrior scream. It was filled with pent-up anger and frustration over the decades and decades of abuse and injustices they felt. The only thing remaining was the squeal of tires and dust in the air.

Isabel and the others let out a sigh of relief. They stood there a moment to compose themselves. As they glanced around the tribe to ensure everyone was OK, a sadness settled over the women. They hugged each other, and for her safety, they directed Isabel to park Van Go in an area reserved for their tribe. Suddenly, one of their female elders appeared, and they instinctively knew to follow her. As they gathered at her feet, she cleared her throat before speaking.

"These are chaotic times we are living in with much change in the air. Most people do not like change because it creates fear inside of them. Fear of the unknown. Fear of loss. Fear of pain. Fear of not having enough for themselves or their families. What you witnessed today was fear, expressed as racism. Do not let their fear turn your heart toward hate or violence. For then you feed their fears."

Grandmother took a moment before continuing.

At that moment, Isabel remembered the famous words that Michelle Obama said to the world while responding to the hatred thrown at her and the president of the United States, Barack Obama, "When they go low, we go high."

Mrs. Obama did not want the words and actions of others to change who she was as a person. She refused to feed their hatred with more vitriol. Instead, she rose above it and was determined to stay true to herself and her values.

Grandmother continued, "What we have in the world today is an epidemic of fearing one another. The fear is genuine. It brings many men to the point of killing one another. Of killing children. We are watching the old ways of the earth disintegrate and become obsolete. Many cling to the past; they want to return to a 'normal time.' That has never happened in the history of humankind, and it isn't going to happen today. Progress is inevitable."

"When old ways fade, it opens up tremendous possibilities for a future we can all participate in. It will take many courageous people working together to create new and innovative solutions for this world. Let us always remember to focus our hearts on healing and working together." And with that, grandmother closed her eyes and seemed to fall asleep.

Rosemary explained that they honor and listen to their elders with respect. "Our education starts at birth and never ends. Many of our teachings are hands-on, and they are meant to become a way of life."

Maureen added, "We educate our children in our own language and stories to help them understand and never lose our unique identity. Our songs, dance, and music help safeguard our culture to keep it alive."

The group slowly shifted and broke apart to reassemble throughout the festival into their respective places. Isabel wandered around admiring the weavings and other artwork, deep in her thoughts. Grandmother's wisdom provoked an introspection, and Isabel unhappily realized that she was a bit like the angry men, full of anger and probably fear too. She regretted how she had taken her feelings out on her family.

Isabel was feeling lonely and a bit jittery about the earlier confrontation. She longed to be with her family and to feel safe again.

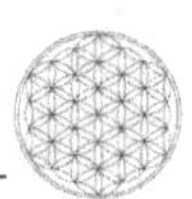

Isabel felt pulled back to the totem pole, and she stood in front of it, feeling the power from simply standing there, being in the presence of the people who created it and who believed in it and prayed that its message would be heard. It moved her in a way that Van Gogh's paintings did.

The carver, Lane, walked over and elaborated a little more on the detailing within the totem. He said, "The two-chinook salmon represent those who are going extinct, those who don't have a voice, and those we must keep fighting for. The diving eagle represents the salmon they are speaking up for. The eagle is a spirit animal symbolic of the power of the Divine, the power of the Great Spirit. Eagle represents a state of grace achieved through hard work, understanding, and completion of the initiation tests, which result in the taking of one's personal power."

He explained that it is only through the trial of experiencing the lows in life as well as the highs and through the trial of trusting one's connection to the Great Spirit that the right to use the essence of Eagle medicine is earned.

His kind words explained that there was also a bear on one side, representing strength and the power of introspection. The wolf, on the other side, represents the pathfinder and one who is loyal to the family. In the middle were hummingbirds to remind us to find the sweetness of life and to open our hearts in all matters to taste the sweet nectar of life.

"The grandmother on the bottom is taking care of both the granddaughter and the mother carved on the other side. Her hand is painted red for Missing Murdered Indigenous Women. Around her were tears representing the seven generations of trauma."

Although Isabel was unsure what God she was praying to, she prayed that the totem pole energy would be lifted to the heavens and the tears that come from it rain down upon the whole country. She prayed that their efforts did not go wasted and become a forgotten episode in time in a few short months.

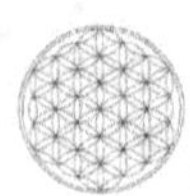

Lane became interested in Van Go and meandered over to admire it. He asked, "Is this beauty yours? Did you create this?"

"Yes," Isabel said proudly.

He went on, "It is always curious to me how people assume that it is insanity and not the vision of another world that made him unable to live in this world. Some people become uncomfortable that a person can even straddle two worlds. Our ancestors knew there was more to this world than we could see with our eyes."

"And because of that, they knew the importance of living in nature and honoring mother earth. We never tried to bend the rules of nature to fit into some unnatural state so that we could simply gain a profit. We knew mother nature only wanted to welcome us to live naturally. Let us never forget; the earth always dominates the environment, and mother earth will reign supreme in the end."

The festival was becoming livelier, and Isabel entertained herself by watching a couple of Lummi artists demonstrate how to carve a beautiful canoe. Surprisingly, they start by carving the outside first. Then they burn out the center. They finish the inside with an axe, using precision cuts. It was true artistry in motion. But they explained that it took an artist, an inventor, and a scientist to figure out how to balance a canoe perfectly.

The canoe races were starting; Isabel found a patch of grass to rest for a moment. After fifteen minutes, she heard music and drumming and wandered to the pavilion to observe their traditional dancing. Their multi-colored outfits of intricate beading could have lived in a museum or art gallery. The Lummi people were obviously very proud of their culture and traditions, and their indomitable spirit permeated the festivities. Isabel felt grateful that these human beings could hold onto their heritage despite all the oppression and abuse thrown at them. Isabel mused about how the human spirit is indeed resilient.

Later she loitered around one of the elders, William, hoping to hear some more words of wisdom. She asked him, "How can you be

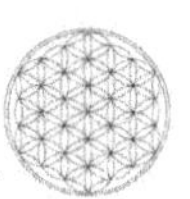

so peaceful or happy inside when so many bad things have happened to you and your tribal nation?"

"The world is full of people with little or no consciousness committing acts of cruelty and selfishness, often with no limits, it seems." He paused for a moment before continuing. "Do you remember the song, *Over the Rainbow*?'"

"Of course! From *The Wizard of Oz*," Isabel said.

"It speaks of people searching for that special place of blue skies and the land they dream of, a place over the rainbow. But how to find this rainbow bridge to connect Heaven and Earth? That's the million-dollar question!" William chuckled.

Isabel said, "That is not the answer I was expecting!"

William continued, "What? You were expecting me to share an old Indian folktale like '*The Two Wolves*? I imagine you've heard of that one?"

Isabel sheepishly nodded her head and said, "Yes, we have two wolves inside of us; be careful which one you feed!" They both laughed, and William said, "Excellent!"

William continued after a moment choosing his words carefully.

"There's a lot of wisdom in our folktales, and people generally need to be reminded of them more than once. The parables lead and assist us to be more mindful in our actions and to choose healthy ways to help us return to balance, most importantly, the balance within ourselves. Our biggest battle is the one inside of ourselves, and it is far too easy to become distracted by the fears inside us. But that misguided focus will only lead us down into an unending cycle of more fear, anger, and violence to be mixed in with the general madness of this world."

"There is a parable called, *The Seven Grandfather Teachings* I'll bet you have never heard. This teaching dates back eons and has always been a part of Native American culture. According to the lore, a messenger was sent to investigate one of the tribes who were living in a negative way. This negative way impacted all of their decisions, thoughts, and behaviors. Some tribal members had hatred for others,

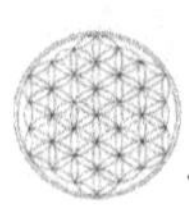

many told lies and cheated others, and some were full of fear and shame. The messenger witnessed disrespectful actions and immense entitlement mixed with too much pride."

"But the messenger came across a small innocent child. This child was chosen to be taught the *Seven Teachings* by the seven grandfathers. He was taught the lessons of love, respect, bravery, truth, honesty, humility, and wisdom. Before departing, the seven grandfathers told him that each of the teachings must be used with the rest. They explained that you could not have wisdom without love, respect, bravery, truth, honesty, and humility. They explained that honesty does not exist without all of the other principles. Because to leave out one would negate the other teachings."

"So, the seven grandfathers each instructed one of their teachings to the child. The child represents us. In order to live a good life, we must faithfully embrace and apply the principles to our own lives. We must also place our trust in the Creator and be sincere in our actions, character, and words."

"What is the difference between truth and honesty? Aren't they the same thing? Isabel asked.

"Truth is when you know who you are in your heart. It will guide your life into right action. Some people call this knowing your true or authentic self." William said.

"I am confused a lot of the time. I feel like I have 30 monkeys inside my head, each writing a Shakespearean tragedy and trying to get my attention. I'm embarrassed to say that sometimes I deliberately do things just to piss off my parents," Isabel said.

"You are taking the time to ask questions and reflect; that is a wonderful start! That is where honesty is important, being honest with yourself, including acknowledging things about your dark nature. You need to do that before you can be honest with others. Just choosing any path of higher intention will lead you in a positive direction," William explained.

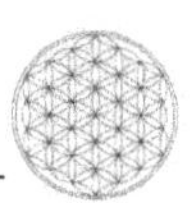

Isabel thought about her mother's words, *'She is at war with herself, but she just doesn't know it.'* She didn't like to think those words were true but couldn't deny the obvious. Isabel had to concede that her parents often gave her excellent advice; however, she found that she did not have as much resistance when the wisdom and guidance came from strangers. *'How unfair of me,'* she thought.

She sighed and said, "You make it seem so easy."

"Living by principles, simple, yes. Easy, sadly, no. Many days I struggle with it. On those days when my personality takes over, you best run to the other side of the camp, duck, and take cover! Or you might find yourself in a shoot-out with me!" William laughed as he must have thought of just such a time before continuing.

"Darkness and light both arose from the source of it all. Darkness is disorder and chaos; Light is order. Darkness transmuted is Light of the Light. Everyone has the power to transmute darkness to light."

Isabel remembered the singing on the bus and how it transformed the whole energy. "I don't think I have quite got the hang of it yet! I seem just to create more chaos wherever I go," Isabel said while remembering her family dynamics of the recent past.

William continued, "Life is messy. We are given free will so that we can learn which way to proceed in life. There will be many mistakes and lessons along the way, but ultimately, you get to choose which path to take. It is not about being perfect or always choosing the correct way; it is about allowing mistakes and then learning from them. A baby can never learn to walk without making mistakes; we too can never learn the higher path without choosing the lower path first."

"If you think about it, you can change a thought instantly if you want to. When you realize how powerful you really are, that will make your soul sing. Your joy and contentment will come from realizing your ability to make a difference in the world." William drifted off to take a nap, much like Grandmother had. Isabel thought, *'It must take a lot out of adults to channel such profound wisdom.'*

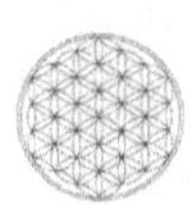

Later that night, they invited Isabel to participate in preparations for their nightly feast. She noticed that everything became a ritual, from spreading the beautiful mats around the fire to slowly cooking the food; every movement was made deliberately and with intention. After they sang prayer songs, they all sat in a circle around the flaming logs eating the sacred salmon and laughing while recounting the day's dramatic events. Isabel felt such a camaraderie with this group of men and women. She admired their bravery and tenacity. She even envied them because they had a tribe; they had each other, and their connection to one another was strong.

When Isabel finally retired for the night, she retrieved the small Tiffany box and gently clasped the necklace around her neck. The emptiness she felt was overwhelming, but she resisted the urge to fill it with food and social media. The People of the Lummi tribe inspired Isabel to fortify her resilience in the midst of challenges. Instead, she imagined herself having the strength of the bear spirit animal and found stillness. The quiet gently overtook everything and her energy naturally moved inward toward introspection. After listening to the mountain cicadas amidst the silence, she finally felt calm. Then a tiny voice inside whispered the wisdom to hold onto from today's events.

She pulled out her cell phone and sent an Instagram post so she would not forget.

A transparent life is a life without moral ambiguities when my heart, mind, and emotions are united in my choices between light and darkness.

CHAPTER FOUR

The Power of One Tiny Seed

Isabel had an idea the following day, so she wandered over to Rosemary and Maureen to share it.

"I think I am going to change my itinerary," said Isabel. "I want to come with you to D.C."

The women became quiet and exchanged glances. Rosemary spoke to Isabel in a gentle, firm voice, "No, it would not be right for you to follow the totem pole to Washington."

She spoke with such tenderness and respect that Isabel found it impossible to argue with her. At the same time, she was a bit brokenhearted.

Maureen continued, "Please understand this is not your journey to follow the Lummi tribe. It is one we have planned for years, and we must follow up on our own. And what message would we be sending if a white girl led us in a milk truck painted with Van Gogh's *Starry Night*?" They all laughed good-naturedly.

Isabel was disappointed but understood this was their journey and their mission. She knew she had just stumbled on a great event and had become a part of it for a short while, but she had to go her way, and they had to go theirs.

The elders bid her farewell while admiring Van Go. "You have created this magnificent piece of art while being inspired by the Great Spirit. You have done well. May you have a safe and powerful spiritual journey too."

They all stood and waved goodbye until she could no longer see them in her rearview mirror. Isabel wiped the tears from her eyes and felt thankful for the experience. She knew she would never forget these brave and proud people if she lived to be 120. Now she wondered how to create a spiritual journey for herself, starting with the Yakima Apple Festival.

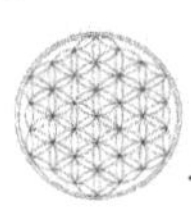

The Yakima Valley Apple Festival was about 175 miles from Seattle. That seemed about how far you truly must be from the city to call yourselves farmers. It was as if the Seattle urban culture of coffee, tourists, seafood, and demographics did not affect the eastern half of Washington.

Yakima Valley boasts about its 300 days of sunshine a year, and today was one of those days. It is also home to more than 18,000 acres of vineyards, lending itself to many fine wineries. But Isabel had no time to drink or sample and instead put on one of her best sun hats to take in the large crowds inside the fairgrounds. She strolled past Yakima Valley SunDome, a 6195-seat arena, which held everything from football playoffs to soccer matches, music festivals, hot tub "Blowout sales!" pro-wrestling extravaganzas, and machinery sale events.

Many people stopped at one of the booths stacked high, groaning from the weight of a dozen different apple permutations, like apple pies, apple fritters, apple cakes, and candied apples on a stick. Mason jars were also full of homemade applesauce, and there were boxes of dried apples, bottles of apple syrup, assorted apple candies, and even apple gum.

Next to those booths were other apple products; you could call it "everything made from apples, natural and otherwise." There were apple T-shirts, apple hats, apple bikinis (consisting of strategically placed apples), and T-shirts that said, *Yakima Valley Orchards is the home of the REAL Big Apple*! There were apple earrings, apple-shaped porcelain clocks, apple-shaped teapots, inflatable apples, a string of tiny plastic apples as a necklace, and the list went on and on.

Isabel followed an ambling crowd to a much quieter side of the fair. That is where the smells and her memories kicked in—crushed apples. The aroma drifted Isabel into her childhood memories of when her family first moved to Portland. Memories of driving up the Columbia River Gorge to Cavender's for fresh apple cider from their large commercial press and "Pick your pumpkins" from the two

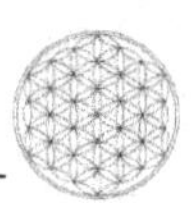

acres of potential jack-o-lanterns. It was an annual delight. It was also next to the terrifying corn maze, only terrifying when she was very young. Then when she was older, the ever-changing corn maze became challenging and a test of skill. They were part of the simple things Isabel loved about Oregon.

Cavender Family Farms was on the 35-mile scenic route of farm after small, family-owned farms, stretched out on route 43, above the Columbia River Gorge and the town of Hood River. Orchards and vineyards sold their products primarily in homey roadside stands. It was adorably called "The Fruit Loop." Although there are ten times as many orchards and fruit farms in the Yakima Valley, no one in the Yakima Valley Community of farmers and cowboys would dare call it something as "liberal and snowflakey" as "The Fruit Loop."

There were family farms scattered across the Columbia River in the Yakima Valley in neighboring Washington State, but mostly there was a lot more commercial farming. The climate and topography were an extension, agriculturally, of the Oregon Fruit Loop. But the Yakima Valley was far more extensive and one of the most prolific fruit and vegetable production centers in the United States. Apples, peaches, pears, plums, cherries, apricots, and nectarines grow there.

She saw the people gathering around the open doors of a somewhat rickety, faded, rooster-red barn. The barn had been shabby for as long as anyone could remember since the fair started in 1948.

The barn housed a sizeable wooden apple press, this one far older and funkier than the one on The Cavender Farm. Its mechanics were similar in purpose yet different in construction in the way they built those unique, hand-built apple cider presses. They based it on the carpentry skills of the farmer, make-do materials at hand, and those store-bought parts the farmer could afford, such as the cheerful, industrious clatter of an engine, once a part of a long gone, John Deere diesel-powered piece of farm machinery. It was attached to a flywheel by a long, floppy canvas belt. It spun another flywheel that propelled an axle welded onto a nasty-looking metal barrel with viciously sharp blades that slashed and throttled the apples fed into it by four teenagers. Gravity pushed the wet mulch called 'pumice' down a metal sluice, much like cement from a cement mixer in a cacophony of spinning, grinding, shredding, with noise from wood and metal parts that looked like it was thumbing its nose at any and all OSHA safety rules and regulations. But that was all part of the show. It was fenced off from any curious little fingers and hands by a sturdy slatted fence.

Four hard-at-work teenagers, all clad in plastic rubber gloves and boots, fed apples into the hopper attached to the grinding barrel. Two more used long hoes to spread the now thick, slushy tan pulp produced by the demonic grinder onto a sheet of wet canvas supported by one of a stack of 4 x 6-foot wooden pallets. They then covered the apple pumice with another sheet of wet canvas stained a dark tan by the liquid from the crushed apples. The young workers then centered the pumice under the thick timbers of a massive apple press which, with a creaking groan, slowly compressed all the pallets full of pumice.

The scene filled with the sounds of liquid gurgling down the chute, the orange plastic buckets filling with thick brown juice, a stretch of other workers, old and young, passing on the pails like a fire line, laughing, chatting. Two more teenage workers were grabbing the buckets of cider before they spilled over, replacing them with more pails. Several more muscular boys wearing red and white "West Valley High Rams" football jerseys tirelessly hoisted the buckets and stepped up three wooden steps to the top of an immense oak cask like one used to age wine.

They rapidly emptied the gallons and the brand-new apple cider into a gaping, hungry black plastic funnel. With all the speed of the pouring, Isabel noted they didn't spill an ounce.

While all this choreographed cider-making activity was going on, a tall, gaunt man stepped in front of the apple press. He was dressed in a coarsely homespun linen shirt and canvas pantaloons, long gone soft from use and wear. The breaches, assisted in holding up the pants

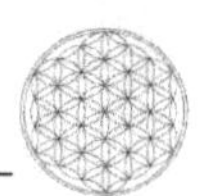

with a rope, were tied around his skinny waist with a half hitch knot. Despite the day's warmth, he wore several shirts and a long coat with huge pockets.

A large, darkly stained canvas sack was slung over his right shoulder. In his left hand, he held a 6ft. long, blackthorn, crosshead country walking stick. Upon his head were hats, yes, plural. One, with ear flaps, was directly in contact with his head. Two more, with brims, sat atop of that, and one, because it was on his head, would be considered, technically, a hat, although it was a battered metal saucepan, which he wore on his head, thus, qualifying it as a hat.

An accurate description of his shoes seems to have been forgotten and fallen between the descriptive cracks. It had not. Although it was impolite to stare, Isabel could not help gazing at his feet. They were bare, although bare could be considered a subjective term considering they seemed to be quite calloused and rough.

His attire and general visage were so dramatic that they caught the crowd's attention, thirstily awaiting the delicious cider. But he waited until the loud, noisy crowd began to quiet down. They became so preoccupied with just who or what he was, muttering quietly amongst themselves (so as not to be impolite) about his unusual attire, demeanor, and how he had positioned himself in front of the crowd, obligated them to look and wonder about him. Isabel sensed they had grown silent and were waiting for an explanation for his unusual and somewhat radical demeanor.

He spoke in a loud but deep and gentle tone.

"You know, in my humble opinion, I reckon there are four kinds of cider; sippin' cider, singing cider, fighting cider, and sleeping cider. I sip, I sing, and I sleep. And, if I do say so myself, I do those three rather well. But I don't cotton to fighting because if a tussle becomes too rowdy, it threatens to spill the cider, and I have observed that it never seems to solve anything. Plus, you miss out on the plain and simple joy of drinking cider with your friends."

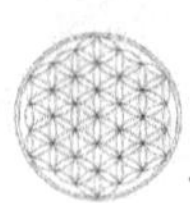

He was nodding and smiling at the crowd, obviously enjoying the attention. They quieted down even more and waited for this man to continue speaking because that was the deal the group seemed to strike between them and this unusual man.

He paused as he pulled himself up to his full height and opened his arms wide to welcome everyone in the audience. "But enough of this jibber jabber... I'd like to introduce myself. However, my introduction is a bit slippery since I have been known not to be called by my birth name, John Chapman, plain and simple. I was born in Leominster, Massachusetts, in 1774. And yes, I do know I look good for my age!" He chuckled softly at his attempt at humor, making the crowd like him even more.

He continued, "I moved to the Ohio Valley, and my goodness, gracious, it was a wild place at the beginning of the nineteenth century. Now my name is a tricky proposition because I am better known in many parts and, in fact, through almost all of the Ohio Valley as Johnny Appleseed. Some folks are more comfortable with Appleseed John. To be honest, I do not mind either one so long as it's used to call me to dinner!" He chuckled so warmly and sincerely at the well-tread, corny joke that it made the crowd laugh too.

'Now I know that some of you think I am a make-believe character, or a cartoon confabulated by Mr. Walt Disney. I can assure you that I am not mythical, as the birth records of Leominster attest. But in the opinion of some very well-respected historians and with much humility and modesty, they wrote that I changed the course of American history." He paused and repeated, "Changed the course of American history."

"Gosh, that sounds awfully puffed up and filled with sinful self-pride. I think it would be more accurate to say I planted a seed (chuckles) which patiently yet powerfully nudged American history; the way the roots of a tree can push aside many things and many obstacles simply by refusing to stop."

"As you can see by all the delicious permutations offered here at this festival, you can eat apples in many ways. They can be dried and used for food in the coldest of winters; you can turn their delicious, sweet cider into the strongest, sourest of kinds of vinegar. You can use that for everything from cleaning and sterilizing wounds to washing and keeping bugs out of your hair to cleaning the rust off your tools, axes, knives, and pots and pans."

At that, he looked upwards and touched the pot on his head. "Oh, yes, speaking of pots. I actually wore a mush pot as a hat, just like this one. I wore other hats as well, so to speak." He pointed to his head as if the crowd had not yet noticed that he wore several hats on top of each other like a stack of pancakes.

"As you can see, I wore them all simultaneously. I believed it was quite efficient in terms of head protection as well as hat hanging, but not quite the 'fashion statement' that I'm surprised to say few, if any, have appreciated for its camping and cooking efficiency," he said with a chuckle.

"Some people thought I was a rather...unique individual. That is a polite way of saying crazy as a bag full of drunk squirrels. I must honestly say that three hundred years ago, America was filled with unique individuals seeking all kinds of freedoms. And I was one of them. How do you put it now? I was considered "off the grid," so maybe a little ahead of my time!"

"Many of us faced all kinds of resistance from people already here. Perhaps that was because we were a new experiment trying to have human beings from all over the world with many beliefs and social, religious, political, and cultural differences simply get along. I see the history of what has become the United States as the constant attempt to figure out just how so many independent, opinionated, and ornery people survive together. I'll be honest. We haven't done such a great job. It isn't easy, and we have made tragic and sometimes terrible mistakes. But I have observed that we're still, despite our streaks of uniqueness and our independent nature, still trying to make it work."

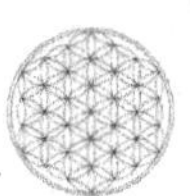

"Many accounts of my life have been written, and many have been completely wrong. It's written in some place in history that I am the way I am because I was kicked in the head by, of all creatures, a cow. Well, OK, that one might be particularly true. And some folks say that led to my vision of planting seeds across this country, but I knew that this country needed the seeds I planted to keep and sustain them. I also knew it would protect them from the harsh conditions the American pioneers settling in the West experienced. And it seemed to the best of my understanding that I was the only one doing this, and many people welcomed me and my seeds into their homes with gratitude."

"Another fact you may find amusing and another reason that many people thought made me unique," he held his hand up and in a stage whisper said, "another way of saying I was loco...was that I was a vegetarian! Now, I hear that's pretty common these days. They even have restaurants for folks like me, but 300 years ago, pioneers would eat just about anything they could trap, hunt with a gun or bow and arrow, or cast a line and catch. They would grow so desperate for any kind of meat that they would train dogs to run a moose into a river, chase it with a boat, jump on his back, hold its antlers, and drown the poor thing! Such was the life of the pioneer."

"As for me, I simply could not kill a living creature which brings me to my next fact, which shocked and worried even more people. I never carried a rifle or any other sort of weapon. I didn't have to because I had two great mothers who showed me where to look to feed myself. Two great mothers, the woman who brought me into this world, and mother nature. God bless them both."

"There are many, many stories which are true. I have to say, about myself and one in particular, about how I crawled into a huge hollowed-out chestnut tree to keep warm on one of those terribly cold Ohio nights, and much to my surprise, I discovered a bear and her cubs asleep, hibernating as it were. So, I left the warmth of the

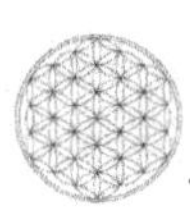

log, and I slept out in the snow. Now, quite honestly, you may think this was entirely noble not to disturb them. But if you know anything about momma bears, it was rather wise that I excused myself!"

"One other time, I lit a fire, and I noticed that bugs were burning in the fire, so I put it out because I would never kill one of God's creatures if I could avoid it. You may ask if I was ever afraid in the wilderness. No Siree! Somebody smarter than me said, *Do not worry about being worried, but accept worry peacefully. And when that becomes a challenge, you pray for the peace to accept it. And if prayer itself is a challenge, you pray as you can, not as you can't.*"

"Now, to get back to why I'm here. My apples. As I said, I am very proud that my apples are known to make three of those ciders. I don't cotton to fighting whether it's because of cider, greed, or intolerance of others."

"Now I have all these opinions, directions, and answers because I abide by the writings of a man who was an inventor, scientist, musician, philosopher, writer, theologian, and mystic, Emanuel Swedenborg. He first wrote a book dramatically titled *"Heaven and Hell,"* which, in his mind, kind of sums things up. He believed that all of us are children of the Universe and that spirits bless us. Yes, I said spirits in all their forms and energies. He believed, and I believe, and more and more people believe in these spirits. You can call them spirit guides, angels, guardian angels, birth angels, and even animal spirit guides, whatever you like; they don't mind at all."

"I believe those spirits are all around us, and you might be able to sense them once you open yourself to receiving guidance. Just try it sometime, sit quietly, and ask for guidance or answers to a particular challenge you might be having. And permit yourself to listen. The power of life lies in the stillness." He paused for a stronger effect and said, "Most people do not allow themselves any quiet time to hear inspiring messages. You might call this meditation, but you don't need to close your eyes or chant. Just take time for quietude. I can guarantee the stillness will not be full of silence!"

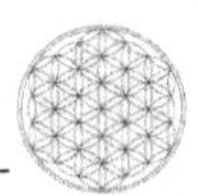

"Your inspiration and guidance might come when you are not even looking for it. Sometimes it can be unpredictable."

"Speaking of unpredictable, I'd like to introduce you to the unpredictability of apple seeds."

He reached into his rucksack and held up one small seed. He said, "This tiny thing is an apple seed. And as you know, I was pretty adept at planting whole orchards of these. But I must tell you all that I have no idea what kind of apple will grow from this particular seed, or any seed for that matter! With all humility, I am an expert, and I still don't know, and neither does any other real expert. Why? The nature of an apple seed is the nature of independence. In other words, if you took this seed from an Empire apple tree and planted it, it doesn't necessarily become an Empire apple tree. It might grow into any species of an apple tree that it darn well wants."

"Potatoes, tomatoes, bananas don't act like this. What you see is what you get with them. But not with the wonderful, independent nature of apples. The whole of the mysterious cosmos is giving us a message. Be yourself, be an independent thinker, and be authentic to your true nature. Just like the apple seed. Just like me, Johnny Appleseed."

The crowd had grown quite large, and Isabel sensed that they were becoming a little bit restless. Johnny Appleseed also noticed it, so he pivoted, "I'm going to stop right now because, with all this talk, I am sure that many of you are thirsty and ready for the apple cider to be served."

Applauding, the crowd all shouted together, "YES!"

He continued, "I thought so, and if you have just a little patience, I will explain how best to receive your delicious cider. Please choose three other people; it's easiest to choose three closest to you. As you form your small groups of four, we will set up the dispensing areas."

The same teenagers working hard on the apple cider press carried small sawhorses to the front of the waiting crowd and placed them in a line on either side of the group. They carefully placed thin plywood planks atop to create makeshift picnic tables.

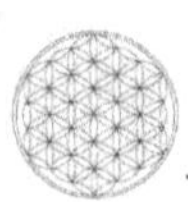

"Now, you decide the one among you who will have the honor of becoming what I call 'the serving host.' There is always one in a group of four who will step up, and the other three can enjoy the respect of being served delicious cider by your new host and friend. Yes, you will become friends because the person will most surely become an immediately grateful friend if served delicious free cider."

And sure enough, the people quickly became groups of four, and they assigned a host who approached the spigots of cider with their trays of four glasses. They promptly filled them and served the other three friends. They all cooperated, and things went amazingly smoothly; you could see the rapport and camaraderie among the groups.

Isabel immediately remembered how the people on the bus gathered together and, through their singing, were able to encourage the impolite man to exit the bus. And in another way, Isabel saw how it happened with the Lummi women with their chanting and singing and how the protestors quickly dispersed back inside their trucks. Isabel thought, '*It reminded me of cockroaches scattering when someone turns on the lights.*'

She approached Johnny Appleseed to see if she might get a moment with him. He turned around and was instantly smiling at her. She hesitated; what to say to this larger-than-normal human being?

"That was a truly great performance you gave. I had to keep reminding myself that I was not hearing the actual Johnny Appleseed. I learned so much too."

The man smiled when he said, "Oh my, I hope it didn't sound like a lecture!"

Isabel flushed. "No, I didn't mean that at all. I meant there was so much fascinating information. It was very entertaining, though."

The man beamed. "Wow. I don't think I've ever gotten such a fine compliment. Thank you."

He extended his hand. "Jordi Lawrence."

Isabel extended her hand and said, "Isabel Hotchkiss. Is this like what you do full- time?"

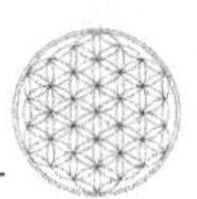

Jordi laughed. "Do I pretend to be Johnny Appleseed all day?"

Isabel could feel herself blush. "Well, not exactly, I..."

Jordi said, "I know what you meant. Sorry, I was just kidding around. But I guess I am Johnny Appleseed because I try to live my life according to many of the philosophies he followed. I am a vegetarian, but I wear shoes but not quite as many hats or pots simultaneously. I started as a regular performer, an actor."

"Oh, have you been in any movies or on television?" Isabel asked.

Jordi said, "Well, unless you were a fan of the soap opera, *Journey to Forever*, you probably haven't seen me before. I'm pretty sure it was on T.V. before you were born."

Isabel asked, "So, is everything you said about Johnny Appleseed true?"

Jordi said, "I believe so. He was a living legend in a time when there were few books and newspapers available to people. Not too many people were literate anyway, so it was pretty much just word of mouth. To be well-known was quite a measure of a person's accomplishments. Even the Indian tribes knew about him. Many believed the Great Spirit touched him. Depending on the tribe, they believed he was either blessed or crazy or both. Either way, it was understood that you left him unharmed even if a particular tribe was at war with the settlers (and there was always a war between the Indians and the settlers). He was considered special and unique."

Jordi said, "I was finished with what I thought was my acting career when this job came along. It wasn't my intention to do Johnny Appleseed for ten years, but it's become a ministry for me. I can say a lot more as Johnny Appleseed than I can as Jordi Lawrence. I can talk about how people can have a better life and maybe help others live a better life too."

"How did you end up here?" Isabel asked.

Jordi said, "By crashing and burning, I guess."

"I don't understand," said Isabel.

Jordi shared, "I knew I was a pretty good actor in high school and college. After I graduated, I went to Los Angeles, just like 5 million other actors every year, to get into film and television. I did better than most right away. My first gig was a Mentos commercial," Jordi gave an exaggerated thumbs-up and a big, toothy, T.V. commercial-ready smile and said, "Mentos, the fresh maker!"

"Oh yeah, I kind of remember those," said Isabel.

Jordi said, "That commercial got me some small parts in sitcoms and then the soap opera *Journey to Forever*. I bought a fancy sports car that I couldn't afford because I thought, '*Hey, I'm on my way to fame and fortune.*' I was also on my way to becoming an alcoholic. Let me put it another way: I was always an alcoholic but never realized it. If you are a certain person, Los Angeles can be lonely even if you're successful. I discovered a big hole in me that I tried to fill with material things, alcohol, then sex, then drugs, but nothing was enough. I burned many bridges by pouring alcohol on them and lighting them on fire. When I hit bottom, I discovered that the bridges I had burned were still burning. I couldn't get any work as an actor whatsoever."

"Wouldn't people give you a second chance? Couldn't you apologize?" asked Isabel.

Jordi said, "I did, but Los Angeles is a tough place. You learn quickly that your reputation is the most important thing you have. A friend of mine said that if the novel, *You Can't Go Home Again* had been written in L.A., they would have titled it, *Do Not Back Up; Severe Tire Damage.*"

Jordi continued, "It didn't take long to run through my savings, and before I knew it, I was homeless, living out of my car on the streets of Los Angeles. And by the way, in case you don't know, it's tough to live in a Corvette. But I was not giving up on my dream. I went to another audition. It was a disaster, and they almost threw me out. And when I was back on the street, wouldn't you know, they announced an A.A. meeting right next door."

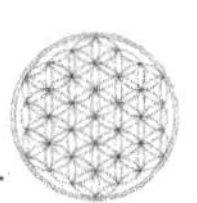

"I don't know why a total stranger stopped and said, *You look like you need a cup of coffee and a donut, want to join me?* Well, he was right. I needed a couple of coffees, a couple of doughnuts, and a friend. His name was Christopher. He has been my friend and sponsor for 12 years."

"The A.A. fellowship is kind of like what Johnny Appleseed did. He kept it simple; he was sober, put one foot in front of the other, talked to people, and planted apple seeds. Three hundred years later, we're still talking about him, what he did, and how he helped people. A.A. is like that. It is amazing what people can do by just talking to each other. No miracle cures, no Pharmaceuticals, legal or otherwise, just accepting and supporting each other. It's a kind of magic, a rock-bottom chemical change."

"The People in A.A. who follow the program don't look for power or control or have any political agenda. In fact, they advise against anything other than helping somebody find recovery. They just sit in a room, talk to each other, and share their experience, strength, and hope. And suddenly, people find that their lives have become transformed. I saw it happen many times down on Skid Row in Los Angeles. All kinds of people from different walks of life become unafraid to look at their actions and motivations that got them where they were. We call it clearing away the wreckage of our past, just people talking to each other."

"Christopher suggested I get a regular job and a practical car. The car was an old Ford Fairlane, and the job was giving away free samples at Costco. Well, I must have still been an actor because this fellow came into Costco, and I guided him to chicken wings while giving him a very entertaining spiel. It turns out he was a major produce distributor in the western part of the United States and needed a fellow to play Johnny Appleseed at a state fair down in Modesto in the Central Valley of California. He even wanted me to write something I could say to the people while selling them his apples. I gave it all I was worth, even writing my script about Johnny Appleseed. It took off, and I began making a living playing Johnny at state fairs, food festivals, and even at schools and libraries all over the country. Pretty

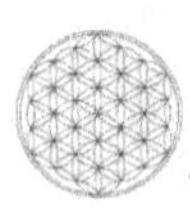

soon, they asked for me, and I spoke at colleges and as you see here at Apple festivals."

"Wow!" Isabel said, "Sometimes you don't get what you want, but you get what you need!"

Jordi laughed and nodded, "I discovered that bringing people together, being honest and open about my past, and sharing my beliefs about love and kindness is magical. People talking to each other creates answers to essential questions. Questions that people didn't even realize they needed to ask. About themselves, the world, and how we hopefully can save it. Save it mostly from our lost souls."

"And you're telling me this happened because you wound up discovering you were an alcoholic and crashing and burning in Los Angeles. And then finding A.A.?" Isabel asked.

Jordi chuckled and said, "Well, that's sort of the short version, but yeah."

"So, what is Skid Row like?" Isabel asked.

Jordi's face became serious and contemplative before saying, "It is the roughest, dirtiest, most desperate, hopeful, heartbreaking, and honest mirror of the world's way of treating human beings that I know of."

Isabel knew she had to go there. Immediately. At least within two weeks as she mentally mapped out a new itinerary. When she shared her crazy idea with Jordi, he insisted she take his contact information as well as Christopher's. He explained that Los Angeles is a big place where you will most surely need a friend. She gave Jordi a big hug and thanked him for everything, especially for inspiring her to be exactly who she is, no apologies, just like Mr. Appleseed and Jordi.

Johnny Appleseed's words stayed with her the rest of the day:

Be yourself, be an independent thinker, and be authentic to your true nature. Just like the apple seed. Just like me, Johnny Appleseed.

She walked off, sipping her apple cider. She was inspired to send an Instagram Post.

You have the power to change the course of history. All it takes is planting one tiny seed at a time.

CHAPTER FIVE

Acceptance and a Little Bit of Puppy Love

Isabel entered the town of Shelley, Idaho, on route 26. She passed by surprisingly modern Shelley High School. In front of the school was the usual announcement board. What was unusual was that the school mascot seemed to be a rather large, tough-looking potato, regally dressed like a king. Emblazoned upon its large portrait was a sign which read, *"Shelley High School-Home of the King Russets."*

It took her a moment to come to terms with the fact the school mascot was a potato, but she conceded that it was a royally tough-looking potato. She considered it might be the only school in America with a potato as its mascot. She slowed to 25 miles per the suddenly posted speed limit and continued on the well-traveled road into the business district. She passed by the town's car dealership, Robinson's Brothers, which was empty and still like a ballroom waiting for an orchestra and dancers.

It was comforting as the houses grew closer together, with occasional churches and businesses occupying the blocks. Isabel loved to see the old, two or three-story early 20th-century homes with their unique architecture and paint schemes. She had a soft spot for their large sunlit rooms, long corridors, and odd creaks and squeaks that old houses invariably have. She wondered who lived in them 100 years ago and if their families were still around.

The town was quiet, but she imagined that most people were at the festival. After the well-kept fire station, she saw a prominent notice on a telephone pole that read: THIS WAY TO SPUD-TACULAR HOT POTATO FEST. The signs sporadically continued on the lamp posts, so Isabel had no problem finding the event. The town did not bother to remove outdated signs announcing *Music Night* at the community center or *Beer and Hot Dog Night* at the local tap.

Isabel thought to research the history of potatoes before venturing into potato country. She found that Inca Indians in Peru were the first to cultivate potatoes around 8000 BC. There are 4373 different types of potatoes, and they come in unique colors of blues, reds, yellows, and even pinks. They also have many different sizes and shapes: small, medium, very large, tubular-shaped, round, and ovals. One Irish potato is named the Lumper potato because it is large and lumpy looking; it is rather unattractive, but it will grow just about anywhere.

Potatoes grow underground in the dirt, or rather the soil, unlike apples, which grow on beautiful trees. Apple orchards are aesthetically depicted and are fun to bring the whole family to. It should be interesting to see how this town makes the potato festival as enticing as the apple festival. But she had to admit, they did a pretty good job with their school mascot, that regal-looking Mr. Potato Head. And small towns generally know how to make spectacular events from the most mundane things.

There was a roster of events planned like the Miss Sweet Potato Pageant, Miss Russet Pageant, The Tater Trot, Spud Run, Car shows, a Potato Pickling contest, Potato Sack races, the Spud Tug, various musical entertainment, free food, and always a parade or two. As silly as most of these events were, they brought the whole community together for a united cause, so they served a greater purpose than who won the best-pickled potatoes or who got to wear the crown this year. They created laughter and memories for all attendees, and it was an excuse to show off your family members to each other.

Even if Isabel did not want to, she made quite the entrance when she drove into these towns. Van Go was hard to miss; she noticed many people stopping, staring, and pointing with open mouths to greet her. A few people waved, but not many seemed excited to meet her. Maybe they don't like outsiders or people who are different. *'Too late to blend in,'* she thought.

Isabel found a place to park and ventured out to explore Shelley City Park and the baseball field where the Spud Tug was going to take

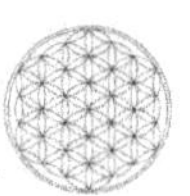

place. Isabel noticed a backhoe digging a square pit in the dirt. A few feet away was a Redi Mix cement truck slowly rotating and stopping every few minutes. A crowd of people surrounded it, surprisingly finding it highly entertaining.

Isabel thought it was strange to have construction happening with the rather large crowds milling around during the Potato Festival. So, she decided to mosey over and see what was occurring around the Redi Mix truck. The driver hopped out, opened a small hatch, and stuck a long-handled tool inside. He then pulled it out to inspect it.

"Almost, not quite," he said.

"Careful, Warren, you'll get paste!" said Joe, the other man.

Warren smiled and said, "23 years, and I've never made paste, Joe, and you know it!"

The crowd seemed to know them both and chuckled at what Isabel guessed was an interplay between the two men that had gone on for a long time. In fact, the whole crowd seemed comfortable with each other, with their easy banter filling up the space. She noticed bleachers several yards behind the cement mixer, and the people were slowly finding their best viewing spot.

But then, the most delicious aroma gently caressed her nose, which instantly took her back to the now-demolished Portland Food Cart Pavilion. The scent was of fried food, more specifically, fried potatoes.

Her eyes then caught the lines forming at 'The Tower of Taters.' It seemed to be a French Fry potato stand unlike any other Isabel had seen. They offered a generous portion of 2 choices from 10 different cuts of French-Fried potatoes for only one dollar. There was the classic French Fry, the Matchstick fries (like McDonald's), thick, breaded logs like Jo-Jo Potatoes, curly fries, tater tots, steak fries, crinkle cut, bistro fries (twice cooked extra crispy), spiced curly, and waffle.

The people filled out their selections before they got to the server, and they seemed to have as much fun filling out the form and selecting their favorites as they did eating the fries. It reminded Isabel of the people waiting in line for her dad's fantastic food. A pang of sadness hit her, thinking about her parents. She thought they probably hated her or were more disappointed in her now because of how she left. She realized she blatantly disobeyed them but also that she needed to create distance to sort out her feelings.

She got in line and ordered Jo-Jo Bistro and Matchstick fries. But at the last moment, she scratched out Matchstick and put waffle fries in their place. The line moved quickly; before she knew it, she had a cardboard box in her hand with the fries expertly divided. Isabel could not believe how good they smelled. She shifted slightly to the left of the line to allow the next customer to order.

She knew she should probably wait a few minutes, but the aroma was too good. She carefully picked one up and blew on it. Baring her teeth to keep her lips from getting burnt, she took a bite.

"Oh, my Goodness, ...these are spectacular! Wow!" Isabel exclaimed to no one in particular.

"First time, I bet," the woman beside her said.

"I've had fries before, outstanding ones, but these..." Isabel said as she continued eating.

"Tallow...beef tallow. It's what McDonald's used to make their fries in. That's what made them so good," the woman explained.

"McDonald's used to be as good as these," someone else chimed in.

"Yes, I believe that is something my dad told me, that they stopped using beef tallow in the 1990s," Isabel remembered.

"Yeah, some Vegan Liberals stuck their big noses into McDonald's business and forced them to stop using beef tallow!" said the big burly man in line.

"I'm sorry; how do you know it was Vegan Liberals that did this?" Isabel said too sharply.

The man narrowed his gaze at her like getting an enemy in his crosshairs. He continued, "Joe Sokoloff, he was a millionaire out of Nebraska. He made his money ripping off people in the scrap business. He even admitted he used his money to bully companies in America to stop using animal fat in their products. I know because it's my

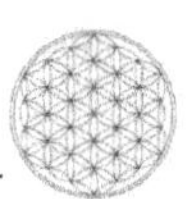

business to know the snowflakes and liberals who are undermining and attacking the America we love, that I love!"

Isabel was taken aback and said, "I love my country too."

The man smirked and looked her up and down before saying, "What you say is often less important than how you say it. I think you sound like a liberal snowflake."

Isabel retorted, "You think? So that means you had a thought in that brain of yours. It must have been a lonely journey!"

Suddenly Isabel felt someone pulling her elbow to guide her out of the path of further word slinging. She looked around to see a kindly woman whose face said everything about not getting involved with that craziness. Isabel let herself be led away as the woman said, "Honey, have you seen the Spud Tug event? It's about to start."

"Thanks for pulling me away," said Isabel as they walked toward the stands. "Those kinds of people just annoy me."

"Oh, Honey, sometimes we all get annoyed around people like that. Thankfully, people like that are in the minority; most of us here are quite reasonable and rational. For those that aren't, well, I have found that people don't change their opinions until they have a particular experience to give them a different perspective. So, why waste your energy? By the way, I'm Margaret."

Isabel introduced herself as she and Margaret walked up to the stands together. They settled into the fourth row. Everyone seemed to know Margaret, and they warmly greeted her. Isabel felt herself relaxing and, at the same time, anticipating the Spud Tug, a tug-of-war contest. Now she understood the construction going on when she entered the park.

"Oh my gosh, that's where they're putting the mashed potatoes - in the trench?! So, the losers find themselves in a vat of mashed potatoes?" Isabel had never seen anything like it.

"Of course! What did you think it was, a swimming competition?" Margaret said.

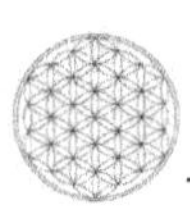

Isabel noticed the various teams with their colored T-shirts. Margaret started pointing out the different squads, like the men and women in the volunteer fire department and their red T-shirts. There were bright yellow T-shirts that spelled out *7 Brothers Ranch and Supplies*. Margaret explained they won the contest last year and have a business in town. There was a team in green T-shirts that simply read, *NRA-Lifetime Member*.

Isabel turned her attention to the people in the stands and saw a few political T-shirts, mostly conservative-leaning, and some derogatory slogans against liberals.

Isabel felt herself getting a physical reaction again. She took a deep breath and said, "I have a hard time being around people who just spew out hatred or intolerance toward someone or a group they don't like or don't understand. You have been so nice to me, and I know the whole town is not like this but isn't it hard to live around intolerant people?"

Margaret said, "I have found a way to walk beside people and accept who they are and where they are on their personal journey."

She continued, "My full name is Margaret Shelly Wilkerson, and my great-great-grandfather John F. Shelley founded this town. I have lived here my whole life and found a way not to take sides over the years. Besides, my father used to tell me; It's better to put your nose in a book than in somebody else's business! It has kept me out of trouble most of the time."

"But what he said about liberals hating and destroying America is not true!" Isabel protested, "How can you not take a side against that stupidity and hatred?"

"I have found when I focus on the dark or the light, I miss out on the beautiful sunset called life. And besides, I just know that I am happier when I assume that people are doing their very best under the circumstances they are dealt with. It keeps me out of judgment and into a feeling of acceptance, rather than on what could be or what should be."

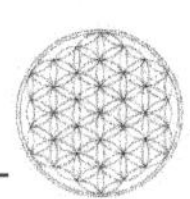

"I have never thought about it that way before," Isabel said, "I don't know if I am strong enough not to have intolerance and hatred bother me."

"Allowing others to have a different opinion than yours is difficult, but not impossible," Margaret said, "The thing about opinions is that everyone has them." (She left out the rest of the saying). "And people generally feel very strongly about their opinions being fact, their beliefs being the only true ones. But if you really think about it, beliefs are the weakest proof of reality. Too many factors influence our beliefs: our cultures, religions, countries, our superstitions, our gender, our families, and even what we watch on television or in the so-called news."

"But I have realized the most important belief is this, *to believe in yourself!* The rest can and will change over time."

Isabel sat there and thought about what Margaret shared. She did seem to be at peace with herself living in this town full of different types of people. She watched as various teams were plunged into the thick, gooey mixture and then hosed off by the fire department. Their laughter was contagious, and Isabel felt herself smiling. But she tired after the third team finished their all-body workout and successfully dragged the losers into the pit of potatoes.

Isabel turned to Margaret and said, "Thank you for helping me and for your words of advice. I feel better now, and I'm going to explore the festival."

Margaret just nodded, "Be mindful. Watch out for any stupid conversations that will just annoy you." Isabel gave her a quick side hug and then climbed down from the stands, saying, "Excuse me," at least eight times as she bumped and jostled people on her way down.

She looked around to get her bearings and then heard a young boy's voice that seemed to float over the crowds cheering and talking, "Belly! Get back here, girl! Belly!"

Then she noticed what must be Belly, a floppy-eared softball of yellow fluff, rolling, stumbling, and weaving its way through the crowd with its leash trailing behind. Its pink tongue was continuously sticking out of its mouth while it appeared she was smiling, wagging her tail, and having the time of her life.

"Belly!!" Isabel saw the young boy trying to keep up with the dog and unsuccessfully stepping on the trailing leash. He was freckled and sweaty and had a look of great concern on his face. The dog looked back but didn't stop. It was heading directly for Isabel, and as it passed, Isabel's old skills as a softball player kicked in, and she scooped up Belly as she ran by. She did not miss a beat as she immediately started to lick Isabel's face. Belly had the unmistakable puppy breath tolerated by those who adore dogs. Isabel, who had never had a dog, was instantly surprised when she discovered she was among the puppy lovers.

The boy reached her moments later and said, "Thanks for catching her, lady."

Isabel smiled at the continuously licking puppy and for being called "Lady" for the first time in her life.

"No problem," said Isabel, "She sure is a cute one."

"Yeah, she sure is. I'm surprised she didn't get taken sooner. Do you want her? She's yours!"

"What?!" Isabel was a bit shocked.

"She's yours. FREE. We dewormed her, and she's got most of her shots. It's Maggie's second litter, and she's the last one. Dad says we've got more than enough to keep the coyotes away."

Isabel was about to hand her back when she heard another name shouted in the crowd.

"Kevin!"

Isabel looked up and saw a man coming toward them. The boy looked just like him, and his father wore a t-shirt from the *NRA for Life* tug-of-war team. She tried to brace herself for the man coming directly at her. Isabel was shocked when he came closer; his face broke out in a massive smile as he said, "She's free, and she is yours to keep. What do you say? Belly is about the friendliest dog I have ever met!"

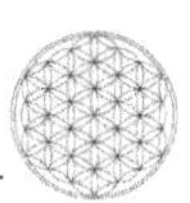

Isabel could not help but smile back. It flashed in her mind that she had done the same thing with Hank. She was assuming things that were probably not true. And that made her smile to think that Hank would find this whole thing very amusing.

"I see that! Why did you name her, Belly?" asked Isabel, stalling a bit.

"Cuz she's got a huge belly!" the boy laughed.

It was true; Belly did have a perfectly round stomach. In fact, Belly herself was a perfectly round ball of fur. Isabel rubbed Belly's tummy as they talked.

"She does have a rather round tummy," said the dad. "But the real truth is we named her after another dog of ours. Best dog I ever had. Her name was Isabel. We called her Belly for short. I know it may sound weird, but we always name the best female dog we give away, Isabel, in a way, as a tribute to keeping our *first* Isabel's spirit alive. Some people keep the name after they hear the story."

"If she's anything like her mom, about the same time she blows her puppy coat, she'll start to get a lot leaner and be a beautiful golden retriever mix, but mostly retriever. Her mom is a smart dog; she sort of trained her a bit. You know, to go outside and not make a mess in the house."

Isabel simply decided to stay quiet about her name. She wasn't sure why, but it seemed it would make things less complicated.

Isabel knew it was a crazy leap of illogical faith, but she thought, '*why not?*' She could not believe the following words were coming out of her mouth, "I'll take her!" Meanwhile, Belly had already decided and was maniacally burrowing into Isabel's neck and hair while licking her ears. She was making puppy noises that Isabel knew could only mean, "I love you! I love you! I love you!" She felt her heart quickly swell when she looked at her.

"I usually ask a few questions just to make sure that the puppies go to a good home, but I saw you sitting with Margaret, and that's enough proof of a background check for me," said the father. "We

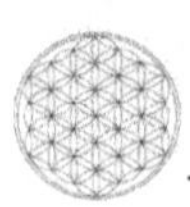

have to go. The tug-of-war for my team is about ready to start. Have a nice day!" The dad put his arm around the boy and walked off, leaving a rather stunned Isabel and the still-licking puppy, Belly.

As she started to walk aimlessly, Isabel's head was spinning with what she had to do now that she had a puppy. *'Ok, ok, first I'll get some dog food. No, wait, puppy food. Right! Puppies eat puppy food. So I have to get a bowl. No, I have plenty of bowls... a bed! Where is she going to sleep? At least I have a leash. And even though they said she was dewormed, yuck 'dewormed'... That is so gross. I should take her to a vet to have her looked at and checked over even though she looks healthy enough... oh my gosh, I don't know why the heck I did this? Maybe somebody will take her.'*

"Isabel?"

Isabel turned and saw Margaret standing there. "Well, my oh my! It looks like you have one of Ben Stanton's puppies. Glad to see he finally gave them all away." She noticed Isabel's face was void of color and full of apprehension, so she asked, "Are you here with anyone or any family?"

Isabel sighed and said, "No, I am here alone, but I am glad you found me. I think I have done something incredibly stupid. I have adopted a puppy, and I am on a road trip, and I really don't know much, anything actually, about puppies, and I don't need a brand new, not trained, or housebroken puppy in a van. I mean, what was I thinking? And I don't have any supplies or food, or bed or anything for her... and, and...." Isabel felt like crying; she was so overwhelmed.

Margaret instinctively hugged Isabel and said," Why don't you come to my house, and we'll talk about it? I take all my cats to a wonderful vet here in town. We can take your cute puppy to her as well. But we will get it all sorted out, and I would love to hear about your road trip!"

Isabel felt relieved and readily accepted. Margaret lived a few blocks away and instructed Isabel to pull into the driveway. If Margaret was shocked at seeing Van Go, she did not show it. She simply admired

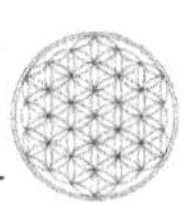

the van and said, "Well, I would love to hear the story behind this beautiful piece of art!"

They went inside while Margaret prepared some lunch and drinks. She later called the vet and set up an appointment for Monday morning, two days away. Margaret insisted that Isabel stay until then to help get the puppy situated and any needed supplies.

"Does she have a name?" asked Margaret.

"Oh, yeah, Belly, short for Isabel!" Isabel said.

"Why, of course, Belly number four... or five, oh, I forget which." Margaret thought for a second and laughed. "My goodness! Isabel and Isabel; it was obviously meant to be."

"Are you sure?" asked Isabel.

"You know," said Margaret, "Things like this always happen for a reason. It's something like how I met my first husband."

"Somebody was giving him away?!" asked Isabel.

Margaret threw her head back and laughed out loud and long." Now, that's funny. No, he was giving some kittens away. And I only took one because he was so cute. My husband, not the kittens, although they were pretty cute too."

Margaret and Isabel spent the next couple of days sharing their stories; Isabel started with Van Go and the process of its transformation. She shared highlights of her journey, such as meeting Hank and how he advised her not to make assumptions about people! She shared her stories of the astounding Lummi tribe, the missing indigenous girls, the totem pole they were taking across the country, and the symbolism. Margaret was an eager listener and marveled at Isabel's experiences so far.

Little Belly was easy to train and was perfectly happy to sleep with Isabel in her bed. She instinctively knew to whine about being let out to pee. On her walks with her, she was a great icebreaker to all dog lovers, and she got to know a few of the townsfolk and many other dogs. All in all, she had to admit the folks in Shelley were a friendly bunch of dog-loving people. There also seemed to be a camaraderie among pet lovers of any kind.

But the most unexpected and wonderful thing happened on the walks; Isabel started to feel the rhythm of something so large, perhaps mother nature, she thought. It was especially noticeable in the early morning before many people were around. She began to feel connected to all things in nature, noticing all the sounds and smells along each walk. Isabel felt everything was alive with some energy that she felt but could not explain. When she slowed her breathing and pace to reflect the rhythm she felt, a sense of peace washed over her.

After Isabel's early morning walks, Margaret always had a cup of coffee and was eager to talk. Isabel was tentative at first about sharing more personal stories about her family because she felt ashamed of how she left them in a fit of anger. But Margaret was so non-judgmental and accepting that it became impossible not to tell her everything. It felt good to talk about her family and how confused she was about why she was so angry about her life and the state of the world. She shared how they call her a "doomer' and the nickname fit.

Finally, Isabel shared what her mom said about her being at war with herself. Isabel wanted Margaret to reassure her and say, "No, that is not true," but that is not what happened. Instead, Margaret took a moment before she asked Isabel what she thought about that statement.

"Do you think it is true?" Margaret asked.

Isabel sat there a moment and then said, "I am not happy with a lot of things like stupid people, and greedy power-hungry people in our government, and all the bigotry and hatred I see, but I don't see how that is being at war with myself."

Margaret nodded and said, "These are not normal times, and there is a lot wrong in our world that needs to change."

She paused and added, "The first step is finding your own peace and serenity. From there, you will make the best choices."

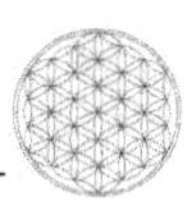

She pulled out a card and said, "This is the serenity prayer; it has helped me to stay balanced."

God, grant me the serenity to accept the things I cannot change, the courage to change the things I can, and the wisdom to know the difference.

"It is a prayer they use in A.A., but I have found it is effective for anyone," Margaret said. "I have found that I can more easily change the things I can when I don't try and change everything. And I cannot stress the acceptance part enough!"

Isabel remembered Jordi and his stories about A.A. and accepting others. Then Isabel recounted all the other synchronicities, like Hank's card and CD of Van Gogh that he shared. And even the puppy whose name was Belly, short for Isabel. She asked Margaret if she could make sense of all her journey's weird and magical experiences.

Margaret listened to all the stories and shared, "Someone once said to me that when you find synchronicities along your journey, it just means you are on the right path. Just keep doing what you are doing. But I think it also shows us that there is order within the universe, that everything is connected."

"Have you heard the saying: *When a butterfly flaps its wings in the Amazon, it can create a hurricane a thousand miles away?*"

"No. Sorry, but that sounds ridiculous," Isabel said.

Margaret laughed and explained, "What that means is we cannot see how everything is connected with our eyes. Most of the time, we cannot even see the effects of our day-to-day actions. But rest assured, we are all connected, and even the smallest acts we perform, good and bad, will have some significant effects on others and the world."

Isabel had to admit she felt something strangely similar to that connection on her early morning walks, but it soon disappeared when her mind became busy, and her thoughts took over.

On Monday, they took Belly to the veterinarian and got her chipped and more supplies. The vet even gave Isabel a short pamphlet on how to train a dog, although it seemed that Belly was already wonderfully self-trained. Even though Isabel felt more confident about her impulsive decision, she was not fully committed to the idea of keeping Belly.

Margaret noticed Isabel's lack of confidence and shared her thoughts, "The only thing this puppy needs is love and attention. You've got this."

Isabel hugged Belly and looked into her eyes. "OK, Girl, if you are brave enough to come with me, I will be brave enough to adopt you for good!" Belly yelped and jumped down and ran in tight circles. They both laughed, and Margaret added, "Good for both of you!"

After a few days, Isabel could not thank Margaret enough and felt strong as she prepared to set off for her next destination. Skid Row was sure to be fascinating!

On the long journey to Los Angeles, Isabel found that she started to talk to Belly. She was delighted that the puppy seemed interested in what she was saying. Every time she began to speak, it hopped onto the other seat and stared directly at her with wide-open eyes, cocking its head as if to say, "Oh wow! That's a fascinating idea, Isabel; tell me more."

Isabel found it easy to talk to the puppy. But then she began to feel guilty because she had not given it a name. Belly, short for Isabel, would not do. Every dog deserves a name; yes, she knew cats deserved names too. Although cats seemed not to care what you called them. Of course, she knew dogs were somewhat the same, but she always felt dogs cared more.

"I'm sorry I haven't named you yet," she said to the dog. As always, Belly cocked her head and waited for her to say something else. Isabel chuckled, "Bella?"

As Isabel looked up to the ceiling, she instantly knew what she would name the dog, the Italian word for a star! "Hello, Stella!" Isabel laughed out loud because when she said "Stella," the dog perked up even more, and she could swear the dog was trying to talk by making little yelping sounds, giving its approval. She was laughing so hard that she started swerving on the road and had to pay attention not to cross the middle line.

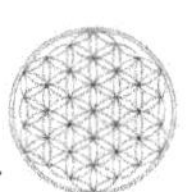

Isabel could see Marlon Brando's famous, torrid scene in which his character, Stanley, ever remorseful after a tantrum, shouts for his wife Stella (Kim Hunter) in Elia Kazan's *A Streetcar Named Desire*. She could imagine her and her father recreating the scene in her backyard as they called Stella inside. That would undoubtedly amuse them and hopefully the neighbors too.

She sent out an Instagram post at her next stop with a photo of her and Stella smiling broadly. The stars were twinkling on the roof of Van Go in the background.

The Stars, Stella, and Serenity; nothing better in this world

CHAPTER SIX

Into the Pit of Despair

Cruising down PCH (Pacific Coast Highway), windows open, cloudless sky, 72 degrees, perfect day, on what should be a glorious drive, Isabel felt a disconnect, a sense of unreality. She was troubled by that. Why was she feeling some kind of nagging, cringy uncomfortableness in her gut?

She had the breathtaking drama of the Southern California Pacific Ocean crashing its white surf on miles of coastline. Looking up at the cliffside, she saw outrageous mansions with multimillion-dollar panoramic views of the sea. And yet, there was something about all of it, something she couldn't put her finger on. For some reason, she could not just enjoy it and say, "Oh, wow! Yes! This is totally cool!"

Briefly, she entertained Benjamin's accusation of her being a "doomer", that she could not just relax and appreciate the here and now.

'Is it true I can't enjoy anything without feeling disappointed that somehow, in some way, this has not met my expectations? Could my idiot brother be correct?'

She thought about how angry and disappointed she was about the trashing of downtown Portland. And the new Lincoln High School. A billion...no, *two* billion dollars, and they get something that looks like the regional office of an insurance company.

And, of course, on a personal level, her total frustration about her completely ignored requests not to have any birthday kerfuffle. Isabel paused her thoughts.

Stella seemed to have the right attitude, sticking her head out the window, taking in the scenery and fresh smells, furiously wagging her tail, and essentially enjoying the moment, the here and now.

'It's just a picture-perfect drive...for a dog,' she thought.

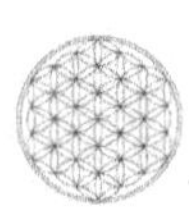

Hold on, maybe that was the reason she was feeling this way. The whole "picture perfect" *perfection* of it all. Yes! Oh my God, yes! Cruising down PCH was like driving through a movie. The entire highway was almost a cliche of 'The Endless Summer' that Southern California promotes and sells to the world. Yes! She was driving in a car commercial! Or maybe it was a light beer commercial, shampoo commercial, or sunglasses ad. It could be for *anything*, just as long as she was driving down Pacific Coast Highway and having the most fantastic time of her life.

The only thing that would make it more of a commercial would be lively travelin' music and voice-over, excitedly intoning: "Take the wheel of your 2022 Electro Van Go…and you're go…go going places!" or "With Imodium, you can enjoy the scenery and forget about emergency stops!" "Feel the wind in your hair and be secure that it's dandruff free!"

Isabel laughed out loud. "Oh, Stella. I am so pathetic!" she said. Stella, delighted they were having a conversation, leaped onto Isabel's lap, licking her face while passionately whining in dog talk, almost making a laughing Isabel swerve again. Isabel quickly put Stella back in the passenger seat and gave her an unearned treat, her favorite. Unearned being the favorite part.

"You're right, Stella. Let's just enjoy exactly where we are. But remind me to get a doggy seat belt for you. And please don't tell your friends I'm a terrible mother… wait! I've got it. Isabel called on Siri to play a song. A couple of seconds later, the famous intro started…, then the lyrics "*Well, East Coast girls are hip/I really dig those styles they wear…*".

Isabel sang at the top of her lungs to blast away the cringy doomer feelings. To her delight, Stella cocked her head and began to "musically" yowl along with her.

If a heart could instantly be filled with love, Isabel's did for Stella. Carefully steering with one hand, Isabel put her arm around Stella and hugged her. "Yes, my love, that's us. We're two California Girls."

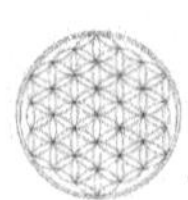

Surprisingly driving a few miles more, she spotted a Whole Foods Market on the left in a small shopping center. The sign made her realize that hunger was calling. She decided it would be an excellent place to get a healthy granola-like snack.

Isabel had "issues" with Whole Foods, especially since the Amazon Gorilla swallowed it whole. But it seemed that, from what she had driven by already, PCH mainly was about small stores selling upscale goods and gourmet restaurants, as evidenced by a branch of Nobu. Although Nobu was one of the best and most innovative sushi restaurants in the world, she was pretty sure it didn't offer a California roll stuffed with trail mix. (Then again, if anybody would try something like a trail mix California roll, Nobu would.)

A few minutes later, as she entered Whole Foods, she realized that they indeed had trail mix; In fact, they had rows upon rows of trail mix, shelves of them, wicker baskets full of them.

'Welcome to Southern California,' she thought.

After what seemed like an hour, Isabel narrowed her selection down to Wild Roots Natural Trail Mix -Coastal Berry Bar Blend and something called Navitas Naturals Organic 3 Berry-Cacao Nib-Cashew Trail Mix.

While overwhelmed with which "organic, natural, hand-crafted, locally sourced, Vegan, unsweetened, fair-trade trail mix to buy, she began to realize that she was standing next to a full-bearded Jim Carrey doing the same thing. She tried to remain very still as if not to scare off the wildlife. But it was unnecessary, as the "wildlife" turned and, with his famous, warm smile, said to Isabel, "Yeah, it's always a tough decision here. Sometimes, I surrender and grab a bag of Tim's Potato Chips." He pointed across the aisle to the well-known red and white striped bags.

"Sometimes I have to remind myself that life is short," he said.

A bit stunned and feeling like a complete dweeb. Isabel could only nod.

"Uh...right...Short," she managed to mutter.

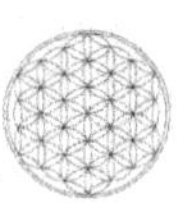

She grabbed a bag of potato chips and a bag of Wild Roots or Navitas Naturals Organic. It didn't matter.

Carrey wheeled away and went whistling down the aisle towards the produce section. Isabel just stood there for a while and then went to check out. She found herself behind a woman talking on her cell phone.

The woman's voice sounded very familiar, like someone she knew. In a way, it was; Jennifer Aniston had a very distinctive voice. At that moment, the voice was deciding whether orchids or lilies would be "just right" for a party she was throwing this evening. All Isabel could think was, '*Oh my God! Her hair and skin really are perfect!*'

Although Isabel knew every episode of *Friends* by heart (and no matter how gorgeous and talented he was, she would *never* forgive Brad Pitt), she felt so mature that she chose not to bother Ms. Aniston.

However, a 1-2 punch of Jim Carrey and Jennifer Aniston made Isabel somewhat giddy. She longed to tell Jennifer Aniston how wonderful she was, but Isabel felt that if she attempted a conversation with the actress, she would have just babbled something idiotic.

Even though she felt she had made the right decision, the incident left her somewhere between dazed, and a bit stressed. She dealt with it by sitting in the van and shoving a giant fist full of trail mix into her mouth, then balancing it with potato chips. Fortified, she continued down PCH into Santa Monica. Driving up the exit ramp from PCH onto Ocean Boulevard, she discovered the exit left her right next to the Santa Monica Pier. The pier extended far into the ocean and seemed the perfect place to clear her head.

The well-known sign over the entrance to the pier looked precisely the way it does in every montage of Los Angeles. It was a bit surreal seeing it in person.

Santa Monica ✦ Yacht Harbor

Sportfishing ✦ Boating ✦ Cafes

Just like her revelation driving down PCH, the large neon sign arching over the Santa Monica Pier made her feel like it was identifying

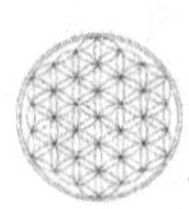

the location she was entering in an episode of a TV series or a scene from a rom-com movie where a couple has a montage of riding the famous merry-go-round, or ferris wheel or winning a giant teddy bear or eating ice cream cones or blah... blah... blah.

Isabel and Stella opted to walk along the path high above the beach instead of navigating the crowded pier. The small park was full of people walking, biking, and sitting on the grass. Stella loved it and lifted her nose to smell the ocean breeze and other dogs. She seemed to make about five doggie friends in five minutes. *'Dogs are simply amazing creatures,'* thought Isabel.

A half-hour later, Isabel found a rare parking spot close to another one of the sites that are a prerequisite for every montage to prove the action is taking place in Southern California/Los Angeles: The Venice Beach Boardwalk and the adjacent sun, sand volleyball players and weightlifters. As she approached it, Isabel discovered that what was universally known as the Venice Beach Boardwalk was not, as she assumed, a boardwalk made of wood, such as the pictures of the Coney Island Boardwalk, Santa Cruz Boardwalk, or the Atlantic City Boardwalk.

The Venice Beach "Boardwalk" was a disappointing, gritty, grease-stained, two-mile-long strip of grubby asphalt, flat on what used to be the beach. Treading along the asphalt was a constant river of tourists. Shorts, t-shirts, and flip-flops were the fashion of the day.

Many people stopped at every funky open-ended store jammed with overpriced junk souvenirs, cheap baseball caps, and t-shirts, primarily items that wound up in garage sales in two years. The stores were broken up by the pizza, fish and chips, burgers, or corn dog stands, most proclaiming that they were "Famous!"

On the beach were jugglers hurling around bowling pins, then bowling balls, and even flaming torches. Amazingly, not to be outdone, there were still others juggling very real, angrily buzzing chainsaws.

They had to compete against one-person bands, two-women bands, beatbox quartets, and card table 'stores' filled with earrings, jewelry,

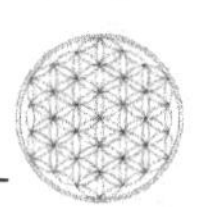

handmade leathers, and weed pipes. There were crazy dancers of all ages competing for 3 minutes of your attention and some small change.

Muscle Beach was in the center and is the open-air weight room for men and women who are not very self-conscious about parading around doing jerks, pull-ups, and other muscular things. Most posers have abnormal bulges that make up their steroidal muscles, bronzed to a deep and dark color like bronzed turkey skin.

Behind them was a steady parade of tourists taking pictures and people who looked as if they were homeless weaving in and out of the photo-taking crowds discreetly begging for money, cigarettes, weed, or food.

For Isabel, it wasn't easy to separate a good portion of them from people who simply lived in the neighborhood. (Isabel judged that the cleaner ones, not the begging ones, were most likely the ones with an actual residence). Stella did not seem to judge them harshly as she wagged her tail and sniffed away at all humans and dogs.

A homeless encampment, like Portland's, was on the thin sandy grass 25 yards away under the palm trees. The ubiquitous shopping carts, piled with belongings, were in front of torn and ragged camping tents or blue tarps, always the same wrinkled and duct-taped blue tarps.

Others slept on cardboard under the palm trees. Some, not bothering with any naptime amenities, were asleep or passed out on the grass and sand.

After an hour, she found herself overwhelmed by it all. She and Stella headed back to Van Go, sat, and turned on the air conditioning. She was incredibly thankful for the solar panels that charged her batteries as she watched the giant, noisy, gritty, kinetic carnival of beach people, tourists, performers, volleyball players, bicycle riders, and shopkeepers. It was a whole churning, stationary circus.

Isabel turned her attention to the vast Pacific Ocean in front of her while listening to the rhythm of the waves crashing on the sand.

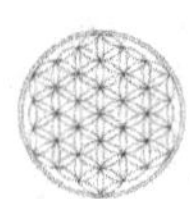

Then she felt that rhythm of the universe similar to what she felt on her walks. She closed her eyes for a moment and did not know she had fallen asleep until she woke up to the sound of Stella barking and some tourists admiring her van.

"Hey, are you part of the Van Gogh Immersion?" someone asked.

Isabel regained her senses quickly. She partially slid open the window.

"Uh, no....Sorry ... I'm not part of that..."

She didn't need to finish her sentence as the group scattered and meandered back to their vehicles. She glanced at the dashboard clock and saw that more time had passed than she realized. Isabel looked at the famous Venice Boardwalk and then drove away, only regretting that she was leaving the ocean.

Following Google directions, Isabel drove down Lincoln Boulevard towards the entrance to the 10 freeway. The screen informed Isabel that the 10 freeway would link to the 110. As she traveled down the 10 freeway, she realized it might be the same tragic-comic freeway O.J. took attempting to pathetically "escape" the 35 cop cars on his tail. Or was that the 405?

'What isn't trapped in a media /movie set in this one-of-a-kind city?' she thought.

She breathed some relief when she saw downtown, Los Angeles. At least it looked like a recognizable city. The 110 deposited Isabel into a construction corridor and new high-rise office buildings.

'Looks like almost every other city in America,' Isabel thought.

Then it struck her that her observation included what developers attempted to do in Portland, Oregon. A kind of heaviness curled up in her gut. She knew that she was mourning the loss of what she remembered as her hometown. She wondered if she was running away from the tearing down and disappearance of cherished places and memories of home. Isabel felt the rumblings of distant turbulence not yet resolved.

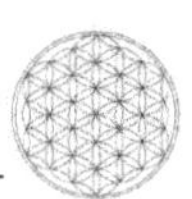

'I think I left a mess back there,' she thought. But at that moment, Isabel had to be aware of another infamous Los Angeles distraction, the traffic. Watching the speeding, swooping, tailgating, insane Los Angeles drivers, Isabel said to Stella, "Holy Cow! They're like a bunch of furiously speeding hornets, and they all drive as if they bought 'Self-Entitlement' insurance."

She drove past the mirrored columns and undulating walls of the Bonaventure Hotel. Built in 1975, it contrasted the after-dark, desolate ghost town of the mid-70s Los Angeles; the Bonaventure was a cutting-edge, space-age architectural marvel.

Isabel flashed to the time when she and her parents were watching one of their favorite movies, *Blade Runner*, and the Bonaventure appeared in the grim, dark, eternal rain of dystopian Los Angeles in the far-off future of 2019.

While the family munched on Phillip's new concoction of buttered garam masala popcorn, he shared one of his famous random facts.

"The Bonaventure has appeared in over 50 movies and TV shows, including *Blade Runner*, *Interstellar*, and *Buck Rogers in the 25th Century*."

The family remained silent, albeit crunching, which prompted Philip to attempt to fill in the awkward silence.

"It's been in more movies and TV shows than most actors."

The memory made Isabel think about Jordi Lawrence, who played Johnny Appleseed. He would find her dad's comments amusing. Then a thought crept into her mind.

She looked at Stella and said, "I should call my parents... or not or...something...oh, I don't know!" Stella simply cocked her head as if to say she did not know either.

She shook her head slightly to get the thoughts out and to focus as a Tesla cut her off; the young female driver, for no apparent reason, shot her a fierce glare and gave her the finger. Isabel thought, *'She's probably wearing a T-shirt proclaiming, Namaste!'*

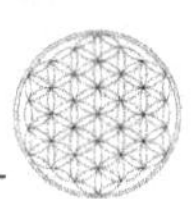

As Isabel drove further into the center of downtown, she decided that Los Angeles was quickly becoming her least favorite city. Too much construction, more high-rises, and flashy but forgettable office buildings assaulted her senses. Then, turning onto 6th Street, Isabel saw something that instantly shocked her. She blurted out, "What the heck?"

Since it was L.A., Isabel's mind went to the idea that she had somehow driven onto a Film noir movie set because she did not expect to find herself tooling down a wide boulevard surrounded by stately old granite and marble banks and office buildings that looked like 1932 Midtown Manhattan. The time travel mystery was solved when she saw a historical marker that read "The Historic Core District."

Later, she would discover the explanation for her head-spinning trans-temporal adventure. When downtown Los Angeles was built in the 1920s and '30s, many "ruling" American architects (born mainly in the late 1800s) dictated that a legitimate and proper downtown business and urban core should look like the Great American cities like Chicago, Detroit, and New York. That meant Beaux Arts buildings were proudly standing, cheek to jowl with late Gothic and Renaissance Revival. And, if they behaved themselves, perhaps they would allow one or two conservative Art Deco edifices in Los Angeles, such as the Title Guarantee Apartments and, of course, the very serious, phallic City Hall.

Conversely, the "Historic Core District" was evidence of the cultural and psychological rejection and abandonment in almost every other part of Los Angeles of the staid, conservative East Coast culture, values, lifestyle, and aspirations. Ironically with all the self-promotion, Los Angeles was capable of, The Historic District is not as well-known nor promoted as Hollywood Boulevard, Beverly Hills, or even Venice Beach. A considerable number of Los Angelenos do not even know it exists.

But for the past 40 years, it has been valued by movie and TV productions as an inexpensive stand-in to replicate downtown Manhattan and many other old East Coast Cities.

"What a disconnected, strange way to live in the city. L.A. seems to be used by the people rather than lived in,' thought Isabel.

Following her navigation, Isabel continued down 6th street. She expected the area to grow increasingly grubby and dangerous, but to her surprise, she passed by a sign that said "Art District-1 mile" It was relatively clean and quiet. Then another sign that said "Fashion District."

'They seem to have to label the districts, so people will know where they are,' Isabel thought.

Isabel noticed many murals in the "Arts District" and only a few blocks away in The Fashion District. Then, as the experience she had of suddenly turning the corner and running into the 1930s Historic District, BAM! There it was. Yet another sign. It made Isabel slightly laugh. Hanging haphazardly on a chain link fence surrounding a vacant lot, a crudely hand-painted sign proclaimed:

WELCOME TO SKID ROW POPULATION-TOO MANY

The traffic light was red, so she had time to look in all directions. The block she was on was as clean as any downtown street in a major city. The sidewalks had a reasonable amount of people walking. However, across the intersection, it was, literally, a different universe. Before she noticed the beer cans and papers littering the streets and trash cans overflowing, she saw the tarps, then rather large tents on every sidewalk.

Isabel *thought* she knew what homeless city encampments looked like, but like everything else about Los Angeles, this was somehow *more*. More traffic, more giant billboards, celebrities, higher prices, and even the number and size of the blue tarps and the camping tents in front of her stretching block by block almost uninterrupted. This was nothing like Venice Beach; this was the epicenter of homelessness in the United States. The sidewalks were overtaken by large tents, leaving any foot traffic to claim what little street space was left.

Stella was wagging her tail, sniffing and whining, and pawing on the window; she wanted to get out and get into the mix of the whole

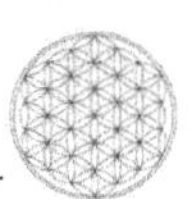

thing and play with the other dogs. To Isabel's surprise, many tent owners also had what looked like a well-cared-for dog. For now, Isabel was quite content to stay in the van and watch the humanity, or lack thereof.

Only a few people seemed to wander aimlessly, dazed, down the crowded sidewalks and intermittently cut across streets, seemingly unaware of the vehicles trying to get by. Isabel expected to see people wearing shapeless clothing that barely hung on thin frames, filthy torn sneakers, or split leather shoes with no laces. Although some wore warm jackets in the 95-degree weather, most people were dressed well enough to blend into any Walmart on a Sunday morning. But juxtaposed against the backdrop of their housing insecurity, one could not help but feel the destitution lurking underneath.

Isabel was shaken by the intense, fatal poverty surrounding her, the apparent unwell population, the raw, sprawling, dystopian, dead-ended-dumping-ground ghettoized and ignored within this city, selling Paradise. When she reached San Pedro Street, she turned left and immediately found a parking spot next to the Weingart Center. Christopher had given her this meeting spot, and she sent him a text message to announce her arrival.

As Isabel took in her surroundings, she realized how different than Los Angeles, the homeless encampments in Portland were, if for no other reason than they existed under the green-leafed, urban canopy of the city's trees and lined the grassy underpasses, brazenly set up in the lush parks, under towering pines, along the bikeways, in the landscapes of median islands with shrubbery separating Portland's "Park" and "Museum" blocks in the center of the city. Oregonians treated trees as sacred, which seemed to extend to the whole population, even the homeless. Despite the invasion of the cold, tall glass towers, Portland was still a lush green urban environment.

Not that Portland's encampments of blue tarps and tents were not shabby and miserable, but the streets of Los Angeles were at a different level of despair. L.A. was built in the high desert directly in

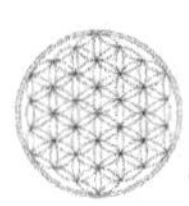

the path of the Santa Ana's, which are hot Desert Winds that bring with them what turns into the city's dust, dirt, grime, and grittiness. Even the first settlers called them "The Devil Winds," which swirl downtown and throughout the metropolitan area an oppressive heat and the relentless drought of the almost year-round summer.

It made Skid Row rough, raw, and ragged, not softened by the pine trees and parks that were such an integral part of Portland, Oregon. The devil winds carried with them the steady thrum of violence. This dark, dangerous energy could explode in a volatile lashing out of charged frustration at any moment.

Isabel opened her windows and immediately felt the heat, the implacable desert heat shimmering up from the asphalt and sidewalks, assaulting the nose with smells of stale beer, unwashed bodies, human excrement, and the sweet rotting garbage of a population simply ignored, simply shut out as efficiently as any oppressed minority. They were left to rot in a no man's land, a war zone hardened by the almost nonexistent Los Angeles River trickling by along with abandoned shopping carts, discarded belongings, and dirty streets: trapped in a concrete sewer.

Isabel was transfixed by all that she was feeling and seeing and smelling, but suddenly there was a bang on her window, which startled her. She jumped. "You got food? You got any free stuff?" a small woman asked while knocking on her window.

'Why does she think I'm selling something or giving something away?' Isabel thought.

Then Isabel caught the reflection of Van Go in a passing vehicle's windows.

'Oh my God! Of course! Isabel, you are a moron!' Isabel realized that the Starry Night mural would signal to people that there was goods or other assistance she was offering the community. Then she noticed at least half a dozen people milling around the van while waiting for her to step out and do something for them. Isabel felt terrible, but she also began feeling a little nervous about telling the

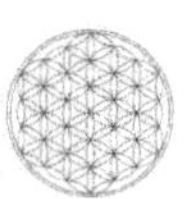

people she did not have anything for them. It didn't help that Stella was barking, whining, and wagging her tail, eager to meet them all.

A loud voice startled her. "Hey, you must be Isabel!" Isabel turned towards the passenger's open window, where she had heard the knock, and saw the face of an older black man bending down and peering in. He wore various crystal necklaces and a rather jaunty wide-brimmed, cowboy-like hat. The man looked to have an official name tag mixed in with the chains. He gave her a big smile and Stella an ear rub through the window. Stella licked his hand in appreciation.

Many people walking by greeted him, "Hey, Mr. Mack!" He returned their greetings by calling many of them by their first name. But he still introduced himself to Isabel, "My name is Christopher Mack."

"Yes, I am Isabel, and this is Stella."

Christopher shook Stella's paw and asked, "How you doin', little friend?" Turning to look at Isabel, "So, you're a friend of Jordi's?"

Without waiting for an answer, he said, "I see you are from Oregon and," scanning his eyes over her van, "that you are probably an artist. Would you like to have a short tour of Skid Row? I don't want you to walk around by yourself trying to see the beautiful sites." He let out another hearty laugh.

Isabel readily agreed and gathered Stella with her leash to explore. Christopher carefully guided her and Stella through the maze of bodies and tents, telling her where to walk. After she talked to him for a while, she found out Christopher was an outreach community worker. His job was to connect the people in Skid Row to various services they might need, including medical, dental, or mental health. She thought the style of his hat was appropriate because Skid Row was, in its own way, the wild, wild west to her.

Christopher pointed out The Weingart Center on the corner. He informed her that they provided temporary housing, support groups, and counseling and served as a halfway house for many newly released people who had been incarcerated. The Midnight Mission was across the corner, and he explained that many people started waiting outside for an available bed that night. They stopped so Stella could meet the small grey suede Pitbull mix named Prince. Christopher introduced Isabel to its owners, Lou Lou and Calvin.

On their way down 6th Street, Isabel walked by several people with small blankets in front of them with various small wares they were selling. Christopher introduced her to many of them. *'How enterprising'*, she thought as one vendor said, "Welcome to Beverly Hills!" She laughed self-consciously because she knew she must stick out as usual with her flaming red hair and freckles, but she secretly hoped she was not overdressed.

They entered the Hippie Kitchen, an outdoor cafe sort of like any ashram setting she had seen in movies. The outdoor garden was serene and a green oasis with picnic tables and a water fountain. Christopher introduced her to the volunteers handing out free food, and they offered her a meal. She felt embarrassed to take one even though she realized she was famished. They were gracious and persistent, so she happily took a vegetarian plate and then a seat in the outdoor area to continue her conversation with Christopher.

Isabel was amazed at how delicious the food was, and Christopher informed her that this organization has been in business for 50 years providing free food for the homeless and underserved populations. He added, "There are some real angels in the world doing good work here on *The Field of Dreams*."

He asked Isabel, "Are you homeless? Do you need a place to stay for the night?"

"Oh no. I came here to see where Jordi used to live, and I don't know why I was inspired to come here, to tell the truth."

Christopher lets out another hearty laugh. "How is Jordi?"

"Well, I think he is doing well. He was working at the Apple Festival up north, and he was awesome, actually."

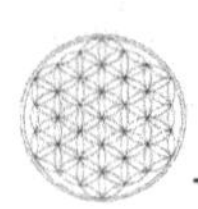

Christopher spoke to Catherine and Jeff, sitting at the end of the serving line, to tell them that Isabel was one of Jordi's friends and reminded them of his volunteer work several years ago. He introduced Isabel to them and said that the Hippie Kitchen was their labor of love. They looked like a couple of older hippies and smiled at the memory of Jordi and probably hearing that he was doing well. Upon discovering that several people knew Jordi, she sent him a text message and a photo of her at the Hippie Kitchen.

"How do you stay so cheerful working in Skid Row every day? Isabel asks. "I think I would get so depressed and angry."

Christopher became solemn and then shared his story. "When I first came to work on Skid Row about 20 years ago, I cried for the first two years. I just kept thinking, what will become of the people? It reminded me of an Elephant Graveyard, where all the old and dying elephants go to live out their few remaining days. It was so painful, and I cried so many tears."

"But then I started to hear success stories of people getting out and doing well. One person told me they got a job, and another told me they got housing. These little stories gave me hope that people can get out of here. Like Jordi did."

"Something wonderful shifted inside me, and I started singing while walking down the street. Every day I walked down here, I always had a song. The singing made me feel better, and I think it made other people feel better too."

"How long are you in town?" asked Christopher.

"I'm not sure. For a few days at least," Isabel said.

"What's the story with your van?" Christopher asked.

"It used to be my dad's food truck. He gave it to me when he opened his restaurant," said Isabel.

"Well, that is a one-of-a-kind van, but you don't want to be here at night, so I would find a place to park it that is safer than here," Christopher said.

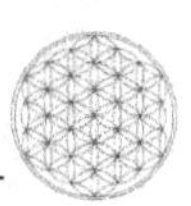

The eating area was bustling now, and Isabel was inclined to jump up and help. Her old working skills in her father's food truck kicked in, and she felt right at home. Catherine and Jeff were thankful for her helping hands and were amazed at how efficient she was. Stella was enjoying their attention while Isabel kept busy. Isabel was surprised at how wonderful it made her feel as she experienced gratitude from everyone. She was reminded of her father's volunteer work in creating the last meals for prisoners and knew that he would be proud of the work she was doing today.

After the lunch rush, Isabel pulled out her cell phone and made a reservation at the Malibu RV Park for that week. The views were spectacular, and it would be a much-needed respite after volunteering on Skid Row. Stella would love the morning walks as much as she would. She committed her time to the Hippie Kitchen during lunch for the next few days and suddenly felt the heaviness of the day fall over her.

Christopher could see that Isabel was a bit overloaded with all the stimulation and suggested they meet back tomorrow so he could introduce her to The Urban Voices Project. He explained that he helped start the community-based choir nine years ago, and everyone is welcome. "I can introduce you to Kate and Leeav, the other directors and co-founder."

He walked Isabel back to Van Go, and she was relieved to be on the freeway again, heading up to Malibu. She marveled at the stamina and fortitude it took to live and work in Skid Row. But she surmised, if you called it *The Field of Dreams*, it must be a labor of love. Isabel could only admire how anyone brought laughter and song to work each day, walking among and through the landscape she saw.

That night Isabel researched the history of Skid Row. She wanted to know how the city got to where several thousand people try their best to create their little place called home with tarps and tents on sidewalks. Isabel snuggled Stella tightly; she found she needed the extra comfort tonight. Isabel's research found it to be a complicated issue and misunderstood by many.

She found that the economic trends and political policies in the 1980s profoundly affected certain people; therefore, homelessness increased exponentially. There were lost jobs due to deindustrialization and, at the same time, a crisis in available, affordable housing. The government cut many social programs; without that safety net, people were now living in or on the edge of severe poverty. Isabel thought, '*What could possibly go wrong?!*'

It did not help that the public's perception of the homeless body was that they were unsightly, smelly, dirty, diseased, and dangerous. The extreme poverty on display made people uncomfortable, so removing homeless people from sight was the city's course of action. L.A. sent the message loud and clear; the homeless body was something dirty that needed to be cleaned up.

Unfortunately, in the 80s, President Reagan announced to the world that people living on the streets made that choice for themselves. The truth was far different than that. Yes, there were shelters, but those shelters became a grueling experience for many, with unsafe conditions such as abuse, theft, and lack of supervision.

She knew at the young age of 21 that these policies were bound to create the disaster she was seeing now. She thought of all the people she met today and tried to imagine how difficult it would be to live your life in public display for most of the day. Their lives are visible all the time, and there is little they can do to create some sense of dignity around a life full of struggles. Many individuals bore scars from their homelessness because it takes a toll on anyone's body.

Isabel fell asleep to the sound of the ocean and the song, *Bridge Over Troubled Water*. She was grateful for her family, friends, Van Go, and soft bed. She felt thankful for Stella and for so many things that she took for granted....until she met others with so little.

True to his word, Christopher came to the Hippie Kitchen the next day to escort her to the Neighborhood Sing. On the walk over,

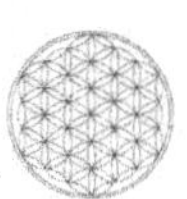

Christopher gave her the latest data from the 2020 Homeless Count gathered on Skid Row. He informed her there were around 4700 people experiencing homelessness on Skid Row, of which 45% were unsheltered. Most were men, and about 75% identified as Black/African-American or Latino/Hispanic. About 35% suffer from substance use disorder, 38% from severe mental illness, and 26% from a physical condition."

"Being homeless is a trauma within itself. And everyone has some form of trauma they are trying to heal that got them to this place!"

"It's like American society has built a maze made of a huge, high, solid wall of racial and social prejudices, technicalities, and circumstances that the people in Skid Row cannot get around, climb over, dig under, or push down and those walls come slowly, slowly together and just crush the life out of these people."

Isabel felt like she had fallen into that dark, black hole of hopelessness again and said, "It all seems hopeless; does anything make a difference? I would not know where to start!"

Christopher said, "That is why so many people do nothing. I believe they want to, but when they first look, all they see is an overwhelming problem with so many issues to address. That becomes paralyzing to many. There are indeed a lot of bad things, terrible things, that are happening here. But there are good things too. People are supporting others, and organizations are contributing in a big way. The sightseers don't see those things by just driving through. They don't see the rich community we have."

Christopher looked at Isabel and paused before adding, "What I now understand is, if you focus on the poverty, the destitution, the mental illness, drug addiction, or any other negative trait, it will lead you down into your own pit of despair. Take it from me. That is a hole that is hard to dig yourself out of. But if you focus on the helpers or how you can assist, that will uplift your spirit. There is a wonderful community down here, more so than in most suburban areas. We take care of one another, and there is always something that we can do, however small, and when we shift to that trajectory, it is life-changing."

"Let me introduce you to The Urban Voices Project."

When she entered the Wellness Center with Christopher, she noticed a rather large gathering of singers and musicians, laughing and talking to one another. There were guitars, keyboards, and other musical instruments scattered about. Christopher said, "Let me introduce you to Bob." Isabel looked around to see who this Bob person might be. Christopher pulled out his Ukulele and said, "This is Bob! He goes to most places with me. I rescued him from a shop in Little Tokyo!"

Just then, Isabel heard a sweet voice singing across the room. It came from a diminutive woman, and she reminded Isabel of a nightingale singing her mesmerizing song. The woman seemed to flutter over to Isabel and introduced herself as Kate, one of the directors.

"Welcome!" Kate said, "Thank you for coming. And who is this fluffy little guy?" Kate bent down to give Stella some ear rubs.

"This is Stella. She is fairly well-behaved; I hope it is OK?" asked Isabel.

"Of course! Everyone is welcome here, and we are fairly well-behaved most of the time, too!" said Kate.

Kate shared that she is a music therapist, and when she moved downtown six years ago, she stumbled upon the Skid Row area. She was appalled and outraged and said, "If I am going to live nearby, I need to do something." It took her one year to build up the courage, and she happened upon Urban Voices one day performing in the park at the annual *Artist Festival*. Everyone welcomed her warmly and invited her to sing during open mic. Kate was amazed at the talented singers and knew immediately that this was the organization she wanted to become a part of.

"Do you see positive results from helping others?" asked Isabel.

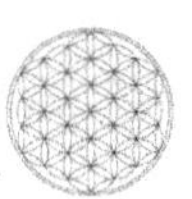

"We feel our greatest mission is to walk with the people and help everyone work together while suspending our personalities. By actively participating in the community, we help alleviate disenfranchisement among people experiencing homelessness. We learned we cannot be anyone's savior, though."

"I see such a wide variety of people here; it certainly is not homogenized!" Isabel said.

"We believe in radical inclusion, and I believe everyone who comes to Skid Row is healing something. When people come into Urban Voices, I try to remember who they are for a moment, whether they came from Beverly Hills or Watts."

Isabel talked to Marilyn, a middle-aged woman with purple hair, flowing clothing, and kind, compassionate eyes. She explained that she suffered a severe fall at work years ago and lost everything, including her home. Although she walked with a cane, Marilyn wanted Isabel to know that she no longer views herself as a victim, nor do her disabilities define her. Instead, she said, "I have an incredible joy for life and feel so much compassion for others, so I dedicate most of my time to being of service."

Just then, Leeav invited her to sing with the choir. Isabel tried her best to back out by saying, "Oh, I can't sing." But Leeav said, "Everyone can sing!" He introduced himself as one of the founding directors. Isabel was surprised he was so young, probably in his 30s, and yet obviously a great leader for this large group. He would not take no for an answer and said to her as he walked away to play the keyboard, "You don't have to be perfect to be amazing!" Kate informed her that Leeav often says that music is the great equalizer. One of the members handed her a personalized songbook with lyrics, and she took her place next to a woman named Roni.

They started with some warm-ups and proceeded with simple songs like, *You are My Sunshine*, and an original piece by Urban Voices called, *Rise Again*. By the time they got to *I Will Survive* by

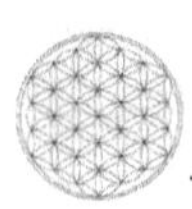

Gloria Gaynor, Isabel was belting it out like a pro. When they took a break, Isabel read the back cover of the songbook:

Urban Voices Project, a 501C3 nonprofit organization. Rooted in Skid Row through music, community, and open-hearted inclusion of the most marginalized members of society, Urban Voices Project amplifies artistic expression to improve well-being, strengthen social networks, and inspire individuals to be their own best advocates.

Isabel remembered her grandfather and how music was so important to him. It was hard to remember when he was not playing, singing, or just listening to music. He often told her in a conspiratorial way that music was what healed the soul, as if he had the secret to the fountain of youth.

After 30 minutes, the choir took a break. Roni immediately sat next to her and introduced the young man with her. "This is my son, Stevie. I adopted him when he was three years old." Stevie had a big smile, and although he appeared non-verbal, his eyes seemed to take everything in. Roni explained that although Stevie looks younger, he is 29 years old and needs constant care as he cannot care for himself. Roni shared that she used to be a professional dancer and musical performer but is now the official sign language interpreter for Urban Voices. "We both feel so accepted and loved by everyone. Stevie loves being a part of the choir; our participation helps improve his verbal skills."

Isabel was impressed with Roni's commitment to her son as she imagined how his life might have turned out with no one to adopt him. Christopher said some real angels were working in Skid Row, but that felt like an understatement to what she was witnessing and experiencing.

A very large, round woman with ultra-bleached white hair introduced herself as Foxy but immediately said, "Upgrade, Holly Golightly." Kate later informed her that Foxy used to be called Shugah and that she changes her name when the spirit guides her.

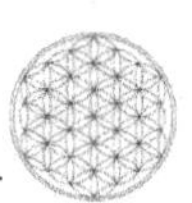

Not to be disrespectful, but Isabel felt like she was in Quark's Bar in Star Trek Deep Space Nine; the range of characters and personalities was so interesting. It reminded her of her eclectic friends from high school, and she felt right at home.

It should be noted that Isabel's 'rather eclectic friends and acquaintances' were an informal band of what was considered geeks, freaks, nerds, outliers, marching band members, goths, skateboarders, gamers, and combinations thereof. In other words, the kids who sat outside or didn't even bother to come into the social landmine of the cafeteria.

She loved how everyone obviously felt comfortable being themselves, with all their unique quirks and artistic expressions. Isabel learned the schedule and was invited back to sing with them anytime. Two days later, she met some more choir members like Franz, who had a silky velvet voice like Nat King Cole. He was timid and humble, and Isabel wondered if he knew how talented he was.

She talked with Iron, who informed her that he is an artist, poet, singer, director, and producer, and since he had the energy of five people, Isabel didn't doubt it. Iron explained that years ago (because he was addicted to painkillers), people severely beat him many times to steal his drugs. His face was still badly deformed from the beatings, and people ridiculed him by calling him Elephant Man. His energy and enthusiasm for life were infectious. Iron said, "Anything to do with creativity makes me soar! Whenever I am awake, I am creating something."

All the voices in the choir were beautiful. But Isabel realized this was not just singing, but beautiful singing from the voices and hearts of a community. She noticed the tight bonding between choir members as they concentrated and explored ways to express complex emotions.

After a few days, Isabel was disappointed that Jordi had not texted her back. At the next choir session, Holly Golightly introduced herself as City. Everyone accepted the new name change, no questions asked.

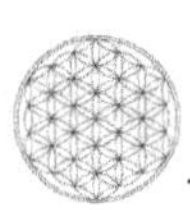

Finally, Jordi texted Isabel back, apologizing for losing his phone. He wondered where she was headed next. She texts back that she is undecided as she did not plan to come to Los Angeles, but she is surprisingly happy. She thanks him for the inspiration.

Jordi texts her that he is doing a show at **"The Living History Farms"** in Urbandale, Iowa. He was hired as a Johnny Appleseed interpreter because they have an Apple Festival called Apple Fest to celebrate the most famous Apple from Iowa: the Red Delicious.

Isabel remembered that Christopher called Skid Row, *The Field of Dreams*. That film brought back beautiful memories, and Philip had talked about them visiting the field someday. Isabel realized that Iowa was calling her to go there next. It was a crazy idea, but so was coming to Los Angeles.

Isabel sent out an Instagram Post with two photos, one of the tents on Skid Row and one of The Urban Voices singing:

From the Pit of Despair to Inspiration and Joy

CHAPTER SEVEN

The Field of Dreams

Isabel woke up early, knowing it was her last day in Los Angeles. She wanted to take a long walk on Staircase beach this morning with Stella before heading out to downtown L.A. Saying goodbye to everyone on Skid Row would be bittersweet, but Isabel felt pulled to Iowa with its vast open spaces, small-town festivals, The Living History Farms, and The Field of Dreams.

While walking Stella, family memories flooded in on the heated debates about what theatrical release would satisfy all members of The Hotchkiss family. It resulted in their missing almost half a dozen screening times. So, Elizabeth insisted that they settle on a stockpile of films they agreed on and enjoyed or tolerated watching more than once. It was not without its rewards because by watching the movies at home, they could share a massive bowl of Philip's latest gourmet popcorn creation.

The movie library included *The Godfather* part 1 and 2 but never 3/*Die Hard*/ *Groundhog Day*/*Toy Story* (several)/*Alien*(several)/ *Titanic*/*The Big Lebowski*/ *Casablanca*/*Indiana Jones and the Raiders of the Lost Ark*/*Back to the Future* (several)/*Men in Black* 1 and 3 but not 2)/*Airplane*/*Beetlejuice*/*Guardians of the Galaxy*/ *Home Alone* (most of them)/*Pulp Fiction*/*Django*/ *Lethal Weapon* (all of them)/and *Star Wars* (all of them).

Then there were the Hotchkiss movie traditions: Isabel, Elizabeth, and Philip loved baseball (Benjamin loved "MVP Baseball 2022" on his PlayStation), so on every Opening Day in Chicago (they were Cubs fans), they would always watch *Field of Dreams* while munching on Vienna brand "Wrigley Field Smokies" (hot dogs) which were served Chicago style (of course) or as they said in Chicago "dragged through the garden" (due to the many toppings) on a poppy seed bun. "Dragged through the garden" consisted of the hot dog topped with yellow mustard, chopped white onions, bright green sweet pickle relish, a dill pickle spear, tomato slices or wedges, pickled sport peppers (a variety of Capsicum annuum), and a dash of celery salt.

Watching *Field of Dreams*, Isabel has favorite secret moments she has never told anyone. It is the times during the film when Kevin Costner hears the voice saying,

"Go the Distance." She loves those points in the movie and always quickly glances at her mother mouthing the words. During these tender occasions, Isabel feels she has a secret private view of her mother's heart.

Other Hotchkiss traditions surrounding watching films are that they would occasionally rent a first-run science fiction movie, but only after extensive research. That was due to Elizabeth's fascination with science fiction stories but only a movie inspired by and rife with the technicalities of science. It could take place in outer space, here on Earth, or even in a galaxy far, far away. It could be about life on other planets, aliens, humans living on Earth and other planets, or science that has gone wrong pretty much anywhere in the universe.

The fun part of watching the ones Elizabeth suggested was that she always mainly remained silent during the movie. The rest of the family would be watching the movie and constantly listening for her "tell," which always came in the form of an almost silent "hmm" or a "pfft" of expelled air. At that juncture, they would pause the movie and ask her what glaring scientific error only seen by Elizabeth had provoked her displeasure.

The dance around their mother's expertise was cute; Elizabeth would always be flustered and apologize for making a sound of displeasure or disagreement. She would hem and haw and attempt to be as tactful as possible, but when pressed, she would take a deep breath and then point out the discrepancy, glaring error, or outright crap the filmmaker was trying to slip past the audience.

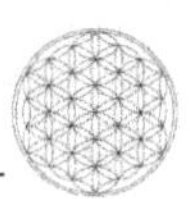

Not only was Elizabeth a brilliant scientist, but she was also a brilliant screenplay rewriter and armchair film editor. Because unless there was such an egregious scientific plot point, she was able to reverse engineer the storyline and come up with some kind of vaguely plausible explanation within seconds, that would allow the family to continue watching the fatally flawed film. She had saved many a movie night.

In his own way, Philip did the same thing with movies about food. Only he was not as quiet or polite as Elizabeth, muttering noisily about what was wrong with the ingredients, the Sous chef's knife skills, or the actor inauthentically portraying the chef. They usually didn't pause the movie for Philip's observations but accepted it as a running commentary.

Isabel happily realized that navigating her childhood memories today brought a smile to her face and warmed her heart. She let out a sigh of relief and prepared for the next leg of her journey. Thankfully Stella would be sufficiently tired for the first part of the drive today and nap peacefully beside her. She scheduled an hour stop in Skid Row to say her goodbyes on her way out of town. *'From one Field of Dreams to the next,'* she thought.

Three days later, Isabel drove into the small town of Adel, Iowa, to attend the Sweet Corn Festival. The first thing that surprised and delighted Isabel on the morning of the festival was that she found a parking spot. She found it with the same kind of ease that she used to find parking spots on the quiet downtown streets of Portland, Oregon, even during the busiest hours.

The second thing that the town of Adel seemed to be gifting Isabel was the massive yet majestic gray stone building that sat like a castle directly in front of her. She parked on the diagonal facing the superstructure. It was smack dab in the middle of one square block of a perfectly manicured, emerald-green oasis of Iowa.

Even before she stepped out of her van, Isabel was charmed by the building's four conical towers with beautifully curved, expansive glass windows capped by round, red clay-shingled turrets. Isabel felt they should have bright and colorful medieval banners snapping in the wind and knights in battle armor protecting the carved archways.

Craning her neck to see the 128 ft. tall clock and bell tower, she was surprised when the bell actually rang a mellow eleven times as the black metal hands displayed eleven. Four giant, square-faced Roman numeral clocks faced all four principle directions. *'Iowa's so flat I bet that people in Minnesota can tell the time in Adel,'* thought Isabel.

Isabel saw the thick brass plaque informing her that the building she admired was: "The Dallas County Courthouse. Built: 1902. Proudfoot and Bird-Architects; Des Moines, Iowa. John Olson- Superintendent of construction. Isabel decided that The Dallas County Courthouse was one of the most adorable courthouses anywhere if courthouses could be considered adorable.

Isabel could also not understand why the courthouse looked so familiar. Then she realized that it looked like Disney had built it and, in fact, it was a very close architectural relative of Cinderella's castle. Isabel would find out later that her artistic eye was correct; the courthouse and the castle were both inspired by French Renaissance architecture. *'Disney should build a new attraction called "Iowa Land,'* she thought.

There was a gentle flow of people walking around the town square on the delightful red brick streets. Isabel noted many teenagers wearing shirts proudly displaying their team's mascot (*Tiger*) and their playing number. Except for the young chattering children who pulled at their parent's arms with excitement, the small groups of people weren't in a rush. Isabel got the sense that they all seemed to be people who enjoyed themselves simply by being around other people.

'Just the same way that flowing water carves out and shapes a coastline, people who live in rural areas have that determined nature about them,' thought Isabel.

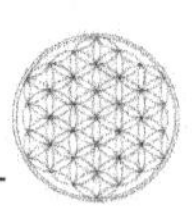

'They plant seeds or harvest crops, depending on the seasons. They work hard in the worst conditions and try their best to protect their crops, livestock, or both, not only because their livelihood depends on it but because that was how they were brought up, handed down generation after generation. It was right and balanced, depending on no one but them. And they know when they are powerless under the green thumb of nature.'

Music wafted around her as she supposed it would be piped into "Iowa Land." There was a sense of calmness, security, and safety in the air. Even Stella seemed calmer, wagging her tail and everybody who walked by. Of course, that may have been because almost everybody who walked by was petting her. Isabel would not have been surprised if there'd be music floating on the Adel breeze if there were no Sweet Corn Festival.

Then she felt a ding of sadness; how contrary it was to the initial feelings of foreboding and danger she felt entering the blocks of Skid Row. Instead of calmness and serenity, the very atmosphere was one of survival. People were on edge because they had lost so much, and their future was uncertain. The disenfranchisement cloaked the air because life did not work out for them the way they wanted or expected.

Isabel remembered how she felt growing up in Portland. It was a city, but a mild one, and her feelings and memories were somewhat like a child might have felt in Adel. From the age of 11, she was allowed to go downtown with a teen neighbor, who was given money for bus fare for both and to have a treat, maybe from Voodoo Donuts or Escape From New York Pizza, then when she was 13, with her friends; casually strolling down Northwest 23rd Street in Portland.

Portland was their world, and that world was theirs. The unique craft shops and bookstores with their goods displayed on the sidewalk, cafes of all types, and exciting new restaurants. She also recalled that, before they gentrified Northwest 23rd, it was ironically the worst part of Portland's Skid Row.

Then she saw a sign that said, *"Adel Sweet Corn Festival!! Celebrating 175 years!!!"* Under it was a kiosk titled *"Information Booth."* Next to that was a sandwich board with "DAILY EVENTS: location, time." Isabel was surprised that the Sweet Corn Festival didn't have the expected carnival rides that most small-town fairs and events had, with the universal group of older men and scruffy teenagers maintaining the ticket booth, crowd control, and clanking thrill rides that most festivals seem to rent from some nameless vagabond company.

She passed the sign announcing, "The Annual Sweet Corn *Concour d'Elegance- Antique Farm Equipment Division."* The quite serious "Judges" (their badges identified them as such) were all in serious navy blue sports jackets with brass buttons, white shirts with regimental striped ties, and straw boaters carrying quite serious clipboards. They were judging massive iron equipment with names such as "Buffalo Springfield," "Massey Harris," and "John Deere." These names were artfully spelled out in flourishes and Gothic script. They were engraved on steel plates proudly bolted to the front of steam-powered wheat threshers, horse-drawn cultivators, and a muscular group of Harvester International, Hager Master, and McCormick tractors.

Isabel watched as a huddle of 5 judges broke apart (Isabel thought they looked like they would soon get into a scrimmage line and a three-point football stance). Then one judge, a large, rotund man with a white/gray beard, who, of course, brought to mind Santa Claus (if Santa also had a long, gray ponytail and sported a bow tie) strode forward with an ear-to-ear grin and placed a luxurious and sizeable blue ribbon on a very orange (according to the sign) *"1948 Minneapolis Moline ZTS 2WD Wide Front Tractor - Owner: Ronald Belgarde."* The judge then shook the hand of, obviously, Ronald Belgarde, who was also grinning ear-to-ear, as all the other judges were patting him on the back and posing for a news cameraman according to his ID badge, "The Des Moines Iowa Register - Video Blog."

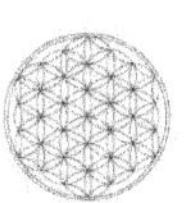

Isabel meandered around the other attractions. Many booths featured local crafts such as hand-carved wooden toys, pottery, jewelry, and macrame. She flashed on all the vendors down on the Venice Beach Boardwalk. '*Not a hash pipe in sight here,*' thought Isabel.

A noisy area of great activity caught Isabel's attention. It was a dynamic group of almost choreographed men and women quickly and efficiently, hoisting yellow plastic milk crates stacked high with ears of corn from a conveyor belt and muscling them towards the awaiting boiling water.

Concurrently, an announcement came over the loudspeaker. "Hello, folks! Free sweet corn will be served in approximately 20 minutes! We promise they'll be enough for everybody, but we ask that you take only two for the first round."

"You know, if you come back next year, maybe we can plan a competition for milk trucks."

Isabel turned, and to her surprise, she saw Santa Claus standing right in front of her.

"Welcome to Adel. Glad you are here," the man said.

Another person walking by called from a few yards away, "Hey, Mayor! Great festival as usual."

Another older man with a cowboy hat walked by and greeted the man, too, by patting him on his back. "How ya doin', governor?"

"Are you the mayor and governor?" Isabel asked.

The man blushed. "Jim Peters, mayor of Adel, and I promise I'm not asking for your vote. That is unless you live here, and I don't think you do. At least I haven't seen you around."

Before Isabel could respond, the mayor kept talking casually, like he had known Isabel for years. "I did see you get out of that magnificent milk truck earlier. What brings you here to our small town; do you like corn that much?"

Isabel laughed and replied, "I am touring around parts of the United States that I have never seen, and Iowa was calling my name." She held out her hand, "Isabel Hotchkiss. Nice to meet you."

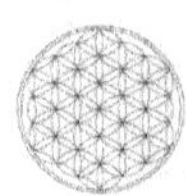

While talking to Isabel, three or four more people said hello across the crowd to Jim. He was able to wave to them and keep talking simultaneously.

"You seem to be a really popular person. That's saying a lot for a politician these days," said Isabel.

Jim laughed, "It's funny, you know, I'm not very political. Most of my issues are stray dogs, junk cars, and tall grass! Our little town has about 6000 people, and I like to say, *there's no place in this town where you shouldn't go.*"

"Every year, we love to showcase Adel to the world, and this little festival draws people like you from all parts. Let me take you to the culinary masterpiece of Iowa."

"Where you from?" Jim asked.

"No place too exotic, just Portland, Oregon," Isabel said.

They took a seat, and almost immediately, Isabel was served a plate with two ears of corn slathered in butter while more people greeted the mayor. She thought, '*It's nice to have friends in high places!*'

"Well, glad you are here!" Jim said, "The Chamber of Commerce started the Sweet Corn Festival years ago as a way to express thanks to its customers. It has become larger than life, with many activities being spun off from it. We now have golf tournaments, the 5K Run, the shucking party, the crowning of the little princess, and lots of musical entertainment. But the best part is the Alumni Association and the reunions every year; we are in our 43rd year. On Friday night, we always have an all-class reunion for any Alumni, and on Saturday night are the prerequisite reunions every five years for various classes."

"Speaking of alumni coming from all parts of the world, here is Dan Norenberg and his wife, Uta. Dan is from Adel, but they live in Germany. Dan's dad, Stan, was principal of Adel High for many years, and his mom was a beloved teacher here."

"How are you doing, young lady?" Dan introduces himself and his beautiful German wife, Uta. "Is the mayor spinning tall tales again? He has been mayor for 31 years, so he has some great stories to tell."

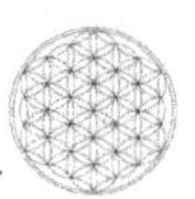

"I am learning all about your beautiful town. I see sports are significant here, like most Midwest towns," Isabel said.

"We believe sports play a huge part in creating healthy, balanced, and successful adults later in life," Jim said. "You are correct; most people are heavily involved, one way or another, and very proud of our teams."

"You know Jim was quite the athlete in his high school years. He was the quarterback of the Adel football team and captain of the basketball team. Both teams made the playoffs, and that's saying a lot for a small town like Adel," Dan said.

Mayor Jim kind of blushed and laughed at the same time. He appeared speechless for a moment, and his humility was endearing.

"Dan could have been a great politician. I should hire him to be my press secretary!" Jim said.

"Hey, sign me up!" Dan replies as they all laugh. Dan and Uta walk away.

"Seriously, have you ever thought of running for higher office?" Isabel asks.

"I have lived here all my life and been married to my wonderful wife Pam for 39 years. We have a couple of grandkids now. My mom, Rosie, used to be the secretary at the High School. My family knows pretty much everyone around these parts, and besides, I love this community; it has everything I want or need."

"I often say, *Is this Heaven? No, it's Adel!*" Jim asked, "You know that movie, *Field of Dreams*?"

Isabel smiled, "It's one of my parents' favorite films. Mine too. That's a big reason why I came to Iowa!"

Jim nodded, "I must have seen that film 20-30 times. I swear, every time Shoeless Joe Jackson asks Ray Kinsella, "Is this heaven?" And Kinsella says, "No, it's Iowa." Jim begins to get watery eyes; he must take a deep breath and pause. His hand went up to his eyes as he wiped them, apologizing and smiling sheepishly.

"Never fails; wife turns and sees if I'm crying again. Of course, I am! Now, I don't know if it's Pam turning to see if I'm crying again or just because I love this town and state so much. But yeah. I cry every time. I'm crying again because of that blessed line."

"My mom's favorite line, and I guess kind of the mantra she lives by, is "Go the... "

"Distance," said Jim. "Go the distance. Yeah. Absolutely."

Isabel thought about her parents watching the movie and how much they enjoyed it. Philip used to say, "Elizabeth? Oh, when she likes something, she is a total head-banging lunatic over whatever it is, as wildly and passionately as only the Amish can be."

Her mom's family was not actually Amish. But close. Elizabeth grew up in Indiana, next to a Mennonite community. Her mother, Naomi, was from a Mennonite family of 11 kids. But when her mom met Carl (her husband-to-be), a race car mechanic on the Bobby Unser team, they joined the Presbyterian Church, married, and started having babies. Isabel loves to hear how Elizabeth honestly came by her mechanical and engineering skills.

Even in the 1990s, her mother fought with her father to be allowed into the STEM program at her school. Like most of the population of northern Indiana, especially Elkhart County, her parents worked at almost all the 30 RV plants in the northern part of the state. When they were old enough, virtually all the next generation worked there too. By age 20, most had experience doing all kinds of hands-on electrical, engine diesel construction, or automotive jobs.

Elizabeth's mother secretly sent an application to Caltech and got Elizabeth an entire ride, one of the finest universities in the world. Caltech saved Elizabeth and got her out of Indiana; she loved every minute of it. Except for the part where she spent four years trying to explain the Midwest to obnoxious East and West Coast physics nerds, the difference between Indiana and Iowa and occasionally Ohio, and the difference between Mennonite and Amish.

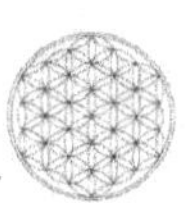

Her mom: the scientist, the genius, and the inventor. A mom who never mentions that she has two Ph.Ds., was valedictorian of her class at Caltech, has four patents to her name, and was the solid rock on which the entire family depended. Isabel knew she was lucky to call her mom.

Isabel thanked Jim for his kindness and decided that two ears of corn were not enough to sustain her for the day. She walked over to Big Al's BBQ and found a seat outside because of Stella. She expected Big Al to be, well, big for one thing. But he was a slim and fit Asian man around 40 years old and just as friendly as the mayor. He started a conversation as he was busily preparing for the lunch crowd by unloading various items from the colossal RV food truck parked in front of his restaurant proclaiming Big Al's BBQ.

"You probably wonder what an Asian man knows about BBQ. But I studied how to make authentic BBQ down south and then started small-time in my garage! Completely illegal, but, hey, look at me now!"

Big Al proudly bragged that Kamilla Harris had stopped and eaten at his establishment. Isabel felt sad she could not enjoy this moment with her dad; he would get a kick out of this place. As she traveled down this particular memory lane, Isabel felt proud of her father with all his kinetic and creative energy around food. She thought, '*Adel is a picture postcard of what a perfect small town in America might be; definitely material for Disney.*'

But as charming as this festival and town were, Isabel's key destination was, *The Field of Dreams*, so she excitedly headed over to Van Go. Isabel briefly read up on the pop-culture tourist attraction in Dyersville, Iowa, and was relieved to hear that dogs were allowed on the field if they were leashed, and their owners picked up after them.

"Stella, you're a lucky dog! You get to experience the *Field of Dreams*." A real pang of guilt struck Isabel. "Oh, Stella, do you realize that we have driven about a thousand miles together, and it has never even occurred to me to find out whether or not you know how to fetch?"

For a moment, Stella adorably cocked her head and seemed to be listening. "I've been selfish," said Isabel. "You are totally my responsibility now. I know I need to ensure you do not run across the highway and you sit when commanded. I know it's better for your brain, and you'd be happier, although you seem as happy as possible without beating me to death with your perpetually wagging tail."

Stella intently looked at her. Isabel would not have been surprised and kind of expected the dog to answer. "Sure! I love to fetch; balls, sticks, and frisbees. You throw it; I'll fetch it!" When they finally arrived, Isabel was tempted to ask the visitors playing catch on the infield (which was allowed) if one of them could throw a baseball for Stella to chase and bring back.

She didn't ask for two reasons; one, because it felt like a breach of trust to let Stella off her leash when the rules specifically said not to; and because if she did unleash Stella and someone was willing to let their baseball be ruined by the saliva of a strange dog (and even though she was a dog lover and adored Stella with all her heart, she was never a big fan of drool). Plus, there was no guarantee Stella would chase it or even bring it back if she did chase it.

And the other possibility would be that Stella would keep running and Isabel would never see her again. Yet, Isabel knew in her heart that wouldn't happen. She knew they had created a bond of trust and love, and Stella would always return. Isabel remembered reading somewhere that until one has loved an animal, a part of one's soul remains unawakened. Those words had no meaning until she got Stella. Now she felt like some invisible thread connected her to Stella, like a strand of electrical energy that couldn't be broken from the outside.

Isabel sat in the stands, and memories unfolded of playing softball on the Alpenrose Field. Her mother and father would watch her play in the Little League Softball World Series every summer. Those were some of Isabel's fondest memories from growing up. She and her father would play catch for hours in the backyard, honing her skills.

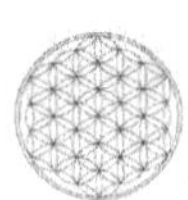

It felt surreal to be sitting here, and Isabel tried to imagine Shoeless Joe Jackson walking out of the cornfield and what he might say to her. She imagined playing baseball with the other imaginary players from the film and how they might compliment her skills of playing. As she daydreamed, she started to feel the enchantment she always felt from watching the movie. Strangely, there was a sense of magic in the air. *'Imagination is one of our superpowers!'* Isabel thought.

Another strange thing happened as Isabel sat watching the players, which had never occurred before. Her mind suddenly went blank. Time seemed to stand still. She realized she was not thinking about anything; she had no thoughts. She became the observer of herself, and a sense of peace quickly enveloped her.

Layers of knowing filled the hallways of her mind, replacing the bogus analysis and misunderstandings that usually took up space. Isabel unhappily realized that most of the time, she was operating like a surface-dweller in the thoughts of her mind. She had only been playing in the minors but had tricked herself into believing they were the majors. Even more painful was the realization that she was often caught up in the ugly dialogue of judging and condemning without looking at herself, her actions, and the consequences of those actions.

Isabel saw how she could not see the silent treasures of her life and that all roads were leading to her self-destruction. There was no choice but to accept these truths, and an unconditional acceptance blanketed her. The ugly truth was that she was self-centered and selfish most of the time. But rather than condemn herself, her heart instantly overflowed with compassion.

Isabel sat there watching the sun slowly start its descent, creating a swirling landscape of color in the vast Iowa sky. She now understood that everyone has the power to become an alchemist; we all have the ability to transform something for the better. She had witnessed this fact over and over again during her journey; so many people she met gave her hope for a better future.

She now saw how easy it is to simply point out everything wrong in the world. But despair and hopelessness are contagious and will quickly rage out of control. Fear can program the mind to do outrageous and illogical things. And if people only bury their heads and ignore issues, it solves nothing and only delays the inevitable. But the simple truth transcends all things, whether we like it or not.

The simple truth was that Isabel no longer felt so pessimistic about the world's future because the people around her inspired her. She saw so much goodness in others as they expanded their kindness and compassion to others. She witnessed all the great Seven principles to live by, over and over again.

'*Go the Distance,*' Isabel heard her mother's voice.

"What?" She shook her head to clear it. She was compelled to look around, just like in the movie, to see if anyone had heard the voice speaking to her. '*That is totally insane,*' thought Isabel. '*They must have little speakers in the ears of corn.*'

'*Go the Distance.*' Isabelle felt a pang in her heart. She knew that in the movie, Ray Kinsella confessed that he interpreted "Go the Distance" to mean he regretted not reaching out to his father to heal the fracture between them.

Isabel looked to the field, and the players laughed and threw the ball at one another, just like Ray Kinsella and his father in the movie's last scene. She suddenly felt the need to wipe her eyes; it seemed they had developed excess moisture. It also seemed that she wanted to hear her parents' voices more than anything.

Isabel rang her father. "Izzy? Are you OK?" Philip waited, expecting the worst.

"Papa? I'm more than OK. I have so much to tell you!"

Isabel smiled and cried at the same time. Everything felt right in her world.

Poem: Nirmana

Alixen Pham is a *Best New Poets 2022* finalist and Best of the Net-nominated poet/ writer/artist with various publications, including *The Slowdown featuring Ada Limon, Salamander, Rust + Moth, New York Quarterly,* and *DiaCRITICS*. She leads the Westside Los Angeles chapter of Women Who Submit, a nonprofit organization nurturing and  supporting women and non-binary writers. Alixen is the recipient of The City of West Hollywood Artist Grant, Brooklyn Poets Fellow, AWP Mentee Program, PEN Center Fiction Scholarship, and others. Her Twitter / Instagram is @AlixenPham.

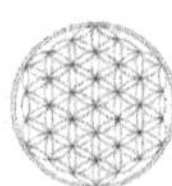

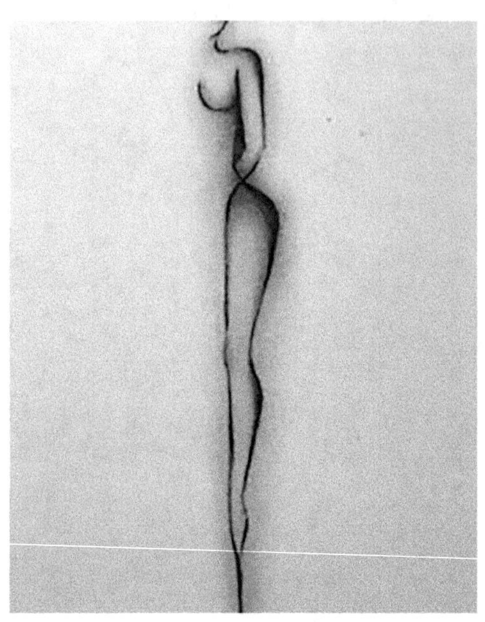

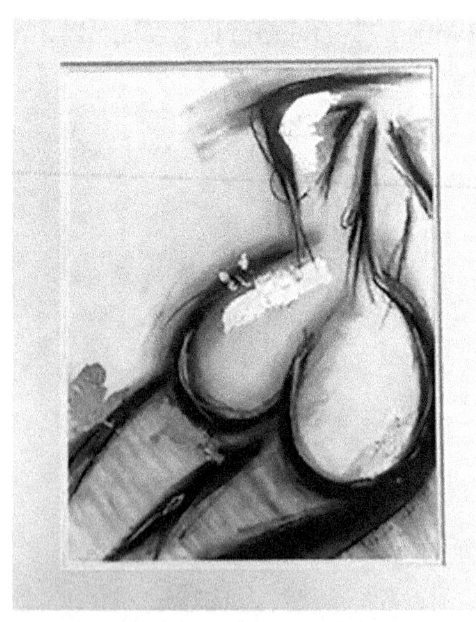

Isabel Artwork

Kristin Jones is a self-taught freelance figurative artist out of Des Moines, Iowa. Born and raised in the Midwest, she was surrounded by a more conservative environment, restricted to the idea that sexuality was something people needed to hide. During the Covid Pandemic, she was able to find an outlet for her expression through art. Her first source of inspiration was Picasso's 'Blue Nude.' She sat on her living room floor and tried to recreate his work over and over until she realized she had a knack for the

female body. Her singular experiment has spiraled into many forms on many mediums with hundreds of buyers.

The Des Moines community has been extremely welcoming. Her work is currently in two establishments in Des Moines and The Ragged Edge Art Gallery in Cedar Falls, Iowa, where she has been the featured artist twice. Her work has even spread west to Los Angeles, where she was featured in Gloria Delson's Contemporary Art gallery in 2021. She will be a showing artist for the second year in a row in Waukee's art Festival along with her first appearance at ArtFest Midwest in summer of 2022.

If you'd like to contact her for a commission piece, please email her at KristinJonesDesign@gmail.com, via Instagram @KristinJonesArt, or visit her website KristinJonesArt.com.

About the Authors

WANDA WEBSTER grew up in Adel, Iowa, and started her career as a special education teacher. She intended to take one year off to "try modeling and acting." That one year turned into 15 years of various opportunities in the entertainment industry, such as an actor, a development executive, and a literary agent. More recently, Wanda returned to her roots in education and obtained a master's degree in Education and Psychology from Pepperdine University. She has since created programs and written curricula for various  companies in the areas of spirituality, social-emotional development, and addiction/recovery with a focus on healing trauma. Wanda works with students with learning differences and continues to develop programs to assist people of all ages in reaching their full potential. She lives in Southern California with her lifetime partner, Christopher Mack, who co-authored their first book, *The Journey Within, How to create the dynamic of recovery to transform your habits and become your authentic self.*

Richard M. is currently writing about himself in the third person and has been a professional writer for 40 years. He is also a grateful member of 12-step programs; hence, for his contributions to Isabel's spiritual journey, his first name and initial will do just fine.

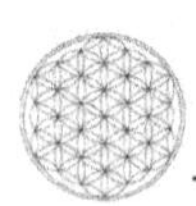

His first paying gig was for a comedy article about his observations coming from New York and landing in Berkeley, California. He submitted it just as a goof to the New York Times. He was shocked when they published it and actually paid him for it. Even more shocked (and pleased) when comedians on TV read it and asked him to write jokes for them.

Since then, Richard has written for dozens of TV shows, from award-winning comedies to documentaries. He's also written songs, novels, comic books, an annotated textbook on Edgar Allan Poe, an Educational TV series on mathematics, interactive edutainment games, a quiz show on grammar, books for American Girl, and even menus. Yep, even menus.

A FEW ANGELS ON SKID ROW

1. The Urban Voices Project: 420 S. San Pedro St. #424 LA CA 90013 www.urbanvoicesproject.org

2. My Friend's House Foundation: 1244 E. 7th St. LA CA 90021 www.myfriendshousela.org

3. Street Symphony Project Inc: 1001 Wilshire Blvd. PMB 2258 LA CA 90017 www.streetsymphony.org

4. Union Rescue Mission: 545 San Pedro St. LA CA 90013 www.urm.org

5. JWCH Institute Inc.: 522 S. San Pedro St. LA CA 90013 www.jwchinstitute.org

6. Studio 526/The People Concern: 2116 Arlington Ave. #100 LA CA 90018 www.thepeopleconcern.org

7. LA Poverty Department (LAPD) 250 S. Broadway LA CA 90012 https://www.lapovertydept.org